COSMIC
KALEIDOSCOPE

COSMIC
KALEIDOSCOPE

BOB SHAW

DOUBLEDAY & COMPANY, INC.

GARDEN CITY, NEW YORK

1977

ISBN: 0-385-12996-3
Library of Congress Catalog Card Number 76-56334
Copyright © 1976, 1977 by Bob Shaw

ACKNOWLEDGMENTS

"Skirmish on a Summer Morning" © 1976 by Bob Shaw

"Unreasonable Facsimile" © 1974 by Aurora Publications for *Long Night of Waiting* edited by Roger Elwood

"A Full Member of the Club" © 1974 by UPD Publishing Corporation for *Galaxy Science Fiction*

"The Silent Partners" © 1959 by Peter Hamilton for *Nebula Science Fiction*

"Element of Chance" © 1969 by UPD Publishing Corporation for *Galaxy Science Fiction*

"The Gioconda Caper" © 1976 by Bob Shaw

"An Uncomic Book Horror Story" © 1975 by New English Library, Ltd., for *Science Fiction Monthly*

"Deflation 2001" © 1972 by Ultimate Publishing Co., Inc., for *Amazing Science Fiction*

"Waltz of the Bodysnatchers" © 1976 by Futura Publications, Ltd., for *Andromeda I* edited by Peter Weston

"A Little Night Flying" © 1975 by Bob Shaw, originally published as "Dark Icarus" in *Science Fiction Monthly* and retitled for *Galaxy Science Fiction*

CONTENTS

COSMIC
KALEIDOSCOPE

Skirmish on a Summer Morning

A flash of silver on the trail about a mile ahead of him brought Gregg out of his reverie. He pulled back on the reins, easing the buckboard to a halt, and took a small leather-covered telescope from the jacket that was lying on the wooden seat beside him. Sliding its sections out with a multiple click, he raised the telescope to his eye, frowning a little at the ragged, gritty pain flaring in his elbows. It was early in the morning and, in spite of the heat, his arms retained some of their nighttime stiffness.

The ground had already begun to bake, agitating the lower levels of air into trembling movement, and the telescope yielded only a swimmy, bleached-out image. It was of a young woman, possibly Mexican, in a silver dress. Gregg brought the instrument down, wiped sweat from his forehead, and tried to make sense of what he had just seen. A woman dressed in silver would have been a rare spectacle anywhere, even in the plushiest saloons of Sacramento, but finding one alone on the trail three miles north of Copper Cross was an event for which he was totally unprepared. Another curious fact was that he had crossed a low ridge five minutes earlier, from which vantage point he had been able to see far ahead along the trail, and he would have sworn it was deserted.

He peered through the telescope again. The woman was standing still and seemed to be looking all around her, like a person who had lost her way, and this, too, puzzled Gregg. A stranger might easily go astray in this part of southern Arizona, but the realization that she was lost would have dawned long before she got near Copper Cross. She would hardly be scanning the monotonous landscape as though it were something new.

Gregg traversed the telescope, searching for a carriage, a runaway or injured horse, anything that would account for the woman's presence. His attention was drawn by a smudge of dust centered on the distant specks of two riders on a branching trail that ran east to the Portfield ranch, and for an instant he thought he had solved the mystery. Josh Portfield sometimes brought a girl back from his expeditions across the border, and it would be in character for him—should one of his guests prove awkward—to dump her outside of town. But a further look at the riders showed they were approaching the main trail and possibly were not yet aware of the woman. Their appearance was, however, an extra factor, which required Gregg's consideration because their paths were likely to cross his.

He was not a cautious man by nature, and for his first forty-eight years had followed an almost deliberate policy of making life interesting by running headlong into every situation, trusting to good reflexes and a quick mind to get him out again if trouble developed. It was this philosophy that had led him to accept the post of unofficial town warden, and which—on the hottest afternoon of a cruel summer—had faced him with the impossible task of quieting down Josh Portfield and four of his cronies when they were inflamed with whisky. Gregg had emerged from the episode with crippled arms and a new habit of planning his every move with the thoughtfulness of a chess master.

The situation before him now did not seem dangerous, but it contained too many unknown factors for his liking. He took his shotgun from the floor of the buckboard, loaded it with two dully rattling shells, and snicked the hammers back. Swearing at the clumsy stiffness of his arms, he slipped the gun into the rawhide loops that were nailed to the underside of the buckboard's seat. It was a dangerous arrangement, not good firearms practice, but the hazard would be greatest for anyone who chose to ride alongside him, and he had the option of warning them off if they were friendly or not excessively hostile.

Gregg flicked the reins and his horse ambled forward, oily highlights stirring on its flanks. He kept his gaze fixed straight ahead and presently saw the two riders cut across the fork of the trail and halt at the fleck of silver fire, which was how the woman appeared to his naked eye. He hoped, for her sake, that they were two of the reasonably decent hands who kept the Portfield spread operating as a ranch, and not a couple of Josh's night-riding lieutenants. As he watched he saw that they were neither dismounting nor holding their horses in one place, but were riding in close slow circles around the woman. He deduced from that one observation that she had been unlucky in her encounter, and a fretful unease began to gnaw at his stomach. Before Gregg's arms had been ruined he would have lashed his horse into a gallop; now his impulse was to turn and go back the way he had come. He compromised by allowing himself to be carried toward the scene at an unhurried pace, hoping all the while that he could escape involvement.

As he drew near the woman, Gregg saw that she was not—as he had supposed—wearing a mantilla, but that her silver dress was an oddly styled garment incorporating a hood, which was drawn up over her head. She was turning this way and that as the riders moved around her. Gregg transferred his attention to the two men and, with a pang of unhappiness, recognized Wolf Caley and Siggy Sorenson. Caley's gray hair and white beard belied the fact that he possessed all the raw appetites and instincts of a young heathen, and as always he had an old fifty-four-bore Tranter shoved into his belt. Sorenson, a thick-set Swedish ex-miner of about thirty, was not wearing a gun, but that scarcely mattered because he had all the lethality of a firearm built into his massive limbs. Both men had been members of the group which, two years earlier, had punished Gregg for meddling in Portfield affairs. They pretended not to notice Gregg's approach, but continually circled the woman, occasionally leaning sideways in their saddles and trying to snatch the silver hood back from her face. Gregg pulled to a halt a few yards from them.

"What are you boys playing at?" he said in conversational tones. The woman turned toward him as soon as he spoke and he glimpsed the pale, haunted oval of her face. The sudden movement caused the unusual silver garment to tighten against her body, and Gregg was shocked to realize that she was in a late stage of pregnancy.

"Go away, Billy boy," Caley said carelessly, without turning his head.

"I think you should leave the lady alone."

"I think you must like the sound of your own bones a-breakin'," Caley replied. He made another grab for the woman's hood, and she ducked to avoid his hand.

"Now cut that out, Wolf." Gregg directed his gaze at the woman. "I'm sorry about this, ma'am. If you're going into town you can ride with me."

"Town? Ride?" Her voice was low and strangely accented. "You are English?"

Gregg had time to wonder why anybody should suspect him of being English rather than American merely because he spoke English. Then Caley moved into the intervening space.

"Stay out of this, Billy boy," he said. "We know how to deal with Mexicans who sneak over the line."

"She isn't Mexican."

"Who asked you?" Caley said irritably, his hand straying to the butt of the Tranter.

Sorenson wheeled his horse out of the circle, came alongside the buckboard, and looked in the back. His eyes widened as he saw the eight stone jars bedded in straw.

"Look here, Wolf," he called. "Mr. Gregg is takin' a whole parcel of his best *pulque* into town. We got us all the makin's of a good party here."

Caley turned to him at once, his bearded face looking almost benign. "Hand me one of those crocks."

Gregg slid his right hand under the buckboard's seat. "It'll cost you eight-fifty."

"I'm not payin' eight-fifty for no cactus juice." Caley shook his head as he urged his horse a little closer to the buckboard, coming almost into line with its transverse seat.

"That's what I get from Whalley's, but I tell you what I'll do," Gregg said reasonably. "I'll let you have a jar each on account and you can have yourselves a drink while I take the lady into town. It's obvious she's lost and . . ." Gregg stopped speaking as he saw that he had completely misjudged Caley's mood.

"Who do you think you are?" Caley demanded. "Talkin' to me like I was a kid! If I'd had my way I'd have finished you off a couple of years back, Gregg. In fact . . ." Caley's mouth compressed until it was visible only as a yellow stain on his white beard, and his china-blue eyes brightened with purpose. His hand was now full on the butt of the Tranter and, even though he had not drawn, his thumb was pulling the hammer back.

Gregg glanced around the shimmering, silent landscape, at the impersonal backdrop of the Sierra Madre, and he knew he had perhaps only one second left in which to make a decision and act on it. Caley had not come fully into line with the hidden shotgun, and as he was still on horseback he was far too high above the muzzle, but Gregg had no other resort. Forcing the calcified knot of his elbow to bend to his will, he managed to reach the shotgun's forward trigger and squeeze it hard. In the last instant Caley seemed to guess what was happening, and he tried to throw himself to one side. There was a thunderous blast and the tightly bunched swarm of pellets ripped through his riding boot, just above the ankle, before plowing a bloody furrow across his horse's rear flank. The terrified animal reared up through a cloud of black gunsmoke, its eyes flaring whitely, and fell sideways with Caley still in the saddle. Gregg heard the sickening crack of a major bone breaking, then Caley began to scream.

"Don't!" Sorenson shouted from the back of his plunging mare. "Don't shoot!" He dug his spurs into the animal's side, rode about fifty yards, and stopped with his hands in the air.

Gregg stared at him blankly for a moment before realizing that —because of the noise, smoke, and confusion—the Swede had no idea of what had happened, nor of how vulnerable Gregg actually was. Caley's continued bellowing as the fallen horse struggled to get off him made it difficult for Gregg to think clearly. The enigmatic woman had drawn her shoulders up and was standing with her hands pressed over her face.

"Stay back there," Gregg shouted to Sorenson before turning to the woman. "Come on—we'd best get out of here."

She began to shiver violently, but made no move toward him. Gregg jumped down from his seat, pulled the shotgun out of its sling, went to the woman, and drew her toward the buckboard. She came submissively and allowed him to help her up into the seat. Gregg heard hoofbeats close behind him and spun around to see that Caley's horse had gotten free and was galloping away to the east, in the direction of the Portfield ranch. Caley was lying clutching a misshapen thigh. He had stopped screaming and seemed to be getting control of himself. Gregg went to him and, as a precaution, knelt and pulled the heavy five-shot pistol from the injured man's belt. It was still cocked.

"You're lucky this didn't go off," Gregg said, carefully lowering the hammer and tucking the gun into his own belt. "A busted leg isn't the worst thing that can happen to a man."

"You're a dead man, Gregg," Caley said faintly, peacefully, his eyes closed. "Josh is away right now . . . but he'll be back soon . . . and he'll bring you to me . . . alive . . . and I'll . . ."

"Save your breath," Gregg advised, concealing his doubts about his own future. "Josh expects his men to be able to take care of their own affairs." He went back to the buckboard and climbed onto the seat beside the bowed, silver-clad figure of the woman.

"I'll take you into town now," he said to her, "but that's all I can do for you, ma'am. Where are you headed?"

"Headed?" She seemed to query the word, and he became certain that English was not her native tongue, although she still did not strike him as being Mexican or Spanish.

"Yes. Where are you going?"

"I cannot go to a town."

"Why not?"

"The prince would find me there. I cannot go to a town."

"Huh?" Gregg flicked the reins, and the buckboard began to roll forward. "Are you telling me you're wanted for something?"

She hesitated. "Yes."

"Well, it can't be all that serious, and they'd have to be lenient. I mean, in view of your . . ."

As Gregg was struggling for words, the woman pushed the hood back from her face with a hand that still trembled noticeably. She was in her midtwenties, with fine golden hair and pale skin that suggested to Gregg that she was city-bred. He guessed that under normal circumstances she would have been lovely, but her features had been deadened by fear and shock, and perhaps exhaustion. Her gray eyes hunted over his face.

"I think you are a good man," she said slowly. "Where do you live?"

"Back along this trail about three miles."

"You live alone?"

"I do, but . . ." The directness of her questioning disturbed Gregg, and he sought inspiration. "Where's your husband, ma'am?"

"I have no husband."

Gregg looked away from her. "Oh. Well, we'd best get on into town."

"No!" The woman half rose, as though planning to jump from the buckboard while it was still in motion, then clutched at her swollen belly and slumped back onto the seat. Gregg felt the weight of her against his side. Dismayed, he looked all around for a possible source of assistance, but saw only Sorenson, who had returned to Caley and was kneeling beside him. Caley was sitting upright, and both men were watching the buckboard and its passengers with the bleak intensity of snakes.

Appalled at the suddenness with which his life had gotten out of control, Gregg swore softly to himself and turned the buckboard in a half circle for the drive back to his house.

The house was small, having begun its existence some ten years earlier as a line shack used by cowhands from a large but decaying ranch. Gregg had bought it and a section of land back in the days when it looked as though he might become a rancher in his own right, and had added two extra rooms, which gave it a patchy appearance from the outside. After his fateful brush with the Portfield men, which had left him unable to cope with more than a vegetable plot, he had been able to sell back most of the land and retain the house. The deal had not been a good one from the point of view of the original owner, but it was a token that some people in the area had appreciated his efforts to uphold the rule of law.

"Here we are," Gregg said. He helped the woman down from the buckboard, forced to support most of her weight and worried about the degree of personal contact involved. The woman was a complete mystery to him, but he knew she was not accustomed to being manhandled. He got her indoors and guided her into the most comfortable chair in the main room. She leaned back in it with her eyes closed, hands pressed to her abdomen.

"Ma'am?" Gregg said anxiously. "Is it time for . . . ? I mean, do you need a doctor?"

Her eyes opened wide. "No! No doctor!"

"But if you're . . ."

"That time is still above me," she said, her voice becoming firmer.

"Just as well—the nearest doctor's about fifty miles from here. Almost as far as the nearest sheriff." Gregg looked down at the woman and was surprised to note that her enveloping one-piece garment, which had shone like a newly minted silver dollar while outside in the sunlight, was now a rich blue-gray. He stared at the cloth and discovered he could detect no sign of seams or stitching. His puzzlement increased.

"I am thirsty," the woman said. "Have you a drink for me?"

"It was too hot for a fire so there's no coffee, but I've got some spring water."

"Water, please."

"There's plenty of whisky and *pulque*. I make it right here. It wouldn't harm you."

"The water, please."

"Right." Gregg went to the oaken bucket, uncovered it, and took out a dipper of cool water. When he turned he saw that the woman was surveying the room's bare pine walls and rough furniture with an expression of mingled revulsion and despair. He felt sorry for her.

"This place isn't much," he said, "but I live here alone, and I don't need much."

"You have no woman?"

Again Gregg was startled by the contrast between the woman's obvious gentility and the bluntness of her questioning. He thought briefly about Ruth Jefferson, who worked in the general store in Copper Cross and who might have been living in his house had things worked out differently, then shook his head. The woman accepted the enameled scoop from him and sipped some water.

"I want to stay here with you," she said.

"You're welcome to rest a while," Gregg replied uneasily, somehow aware of what was coming.

"I want to stay for six days." The woman gave him a direct, calm stare. "Until after my son is born."

Gregg snorted his incredulity. "This is no hospital, and I'm no midwife."

"I'll pay you well." She reached inside her dress-*cum*-cloak and produced a strip of yellow metal that shone with the buttery luster of high-grade gold. It was about eight inches long by an inch wide, with rounded edges and corners. "One of these for each day. That will be six."

"This doesn't make any kind of sense," Gregg floundered. "I mean, you don't even know if six days will be enough."

"My son will be born on the day after tomorrow."

"You can't be sure of that."

"I can."

"Ma'am, I . . ." Gregg picked up the heavy metal tablet. "This would be worth a lot of money . . . to a bank."

"It isn't stolen, if that's what you mean."

He cleared his throat and, not wishing to contradict or quiz his visitor, examined the gold strip for markings. It had no indentations of any kind and had an almost oily feel, which suggested it might be twenty-four-carat pure.

"I didn't say it was stolen—but I don't often get monied ladies coming here to have their babies." He gave her a wry smile. "Fact is, you're the first."

"Delicately put," she said, mustering a smile in return. "I know how strange this must seem to you, but I'm not free to explain it. All I can tell you is that I have broken no laws."

"You just want to go into hiding for a spell."

"Please understand that there are other societies whose ways are not those of Mexico."

"Excuse me, ma'am," Gregg said, wondering, "this territory has been American since 1848."

"Excuse *me*." She was contrite. "I never excelled at geography —and I'm very far from home."

Gregg suspected he was being manipulated and decided to resist. "How about the prince?"

Sunlight reflecting from the water in the dipper she was holding split into concentric rings. "It was wrong of me to think of involving you," she said. "I'll go as soon as I have rested."

"Go where?" Gregg, feeling himself becoming involved regardless of her wishes or his own, gave a scornful laugh. "Ma'am, you don't seem to realize how far you are from anywhere. How did you get out here, anyway?"

"I'll leave now." She stood up with some difficulty, her small face paler than ever. "Thank you for helping me as much as you did. I hope you will accept that piece of gold . . ."

"Sit down," Gregg said resignedly. "If you're crazy enough to want to stay here and have your baby, I guess I'm crazy enough to go along with it."

"Thank you." She sat down heavily, and he knew she had been close to fainting.

"There's no need to keep thanking me." Gregg spoke gruffly to disguise the fact that, in an obscure way, he was pleased that a young and beautiful woman was prepared to entrust herself to his care after such a brief acquaintanceship. *I think you are a good man* were almost the first words she had said to him, and in that moment he had abruptly become aware of how wearisome his life had been in the past two years. Semicrippled, dried out by fifty years of hard living, he should have been immune to romantic notions—especially as the woman could well be a foreign aristocrat who would not even have glanced at him under normal circumstances. The fact remained, however, that he had acted as her protector, and on her behalf had been reintroduced to all the heady addictions of danger. Now the woman was dependent on him and prepared to live in his house. She was also young and beautiful and mysterious—a combination he found as irresistible now as he would have done a quarter of a century earlier.

"We'd best start being practical," he said, compensating for his private flight of fantasy. "You can have my bed for the week. It's clean, but we're going to need fresh linen. I'll go into town and pick up some supplies."

She looked alarmed. "Is that necessary?"

"Very necessary. Don't worry—I won't tell anybody you're here."

"Thank you," she said. "But what about the two men I met?"

"What about them?"

"They probably know I came here with you. Won't they talk about it?"

"Not where it matters. The Portfield men don't mix with the townfolk or anybody else around here." Gregg took Caley's pistol from his belt and was putting it away in a cupboard when the woman held out her hand and asked if she could examine the weapon. Mildly surprised, he handed it to her and noticed the way in which her arm sank as it took the weight.

"It isn't a woman's gun," he commented.

"Obviously." She looked up at him. "What is the muzzle velocity of this weapon?"

Gregg snorted again, showing amusement. "You're not interested in things like that."

"That is a curious remark for you to make," she said, a hint of firmness returning to her voice, "when I have just expressed interest in it."

"Sorry, it's just that . . ." Gregg decided against referring to the terror she had shown earlier when he had fired the shotgun. "I don't know the muzzle velocity, but it can't be very high. That's an old Tranter percussion five-shooter, and you don't see many of them about nowadays. It beats me why Caley took the trouble to lug it around."

"I see." She looked disappointed as she handed the pistol back. "It isn't any good."

Gregg hefted the weapon. "Don't get me wrong, ma'am. This sort of gun is troublesome to load, but it throws a fifty-four-bore slug that'll bowl over any man alive." He was looking at the woman as he spoke, and it seemed to him that, on his final words, an odd expression passed over her face.

"Were you thinking of bigger game?" he said. "Bear, perhaps?"

She ignored his questions. "Have you a pistol of your own?"

"Yes, but I don't carry it. That way I stay out of trouble." Gregg recalled the events of the past hour. "Usually I stay out of trouble."

"What is its muzzle velocity?"

"How would I know?" Gregg found it more and more difficult to reconcile the woman's general demeanor with her strange inter-

est in the technicalities of firearms. "We don't think that way
about guns around here. I've got a .44 Remington that always did
what I wanted it to do, and that's all I ever needed to know about
it."

Undeterred by the impatience in his voice, the woman looked
around the room for a moment and pointed at the massive iron
range on which he did his cooking. "What would happen if you
fired it at that?"

"You'd get pieces of lead bouncing around the room."

"The shot wouldn't go through?"

Gregg chuckled. "There isn't a gun made that could do that.
Would you mind telling me why you're so interested?"

She responded in a way he was learning to expect, by changing
the subject. "Shall I call you Billy boy?"

"Billy is enough," he said. "If we're going to use our given
names."

"My name is Morna, and of course we're going to use our
Christian names." She gave him a twinkling glance. "There's no
point in being formal . . . under the circumstances."

"I guess not." Gregg felt his cheeks grow warm, and he turned
away.

"Have you ever delivered a baby before?"

"It isn't my line of work."

"Well, don't worry about it too much," she said. "I'll instruct
you."

"Thanks," Gregg replied gruffly, wondering if he could have
been wildly wrong in his guess that his visitor was a woman of
high breeding. She had the looks and—now that she was no longer
afraid—a certain imperious quality in her manner, but she appeared to have no idea that there were certain things a woman
should only discuss with her intimates.

In the afternoon he drove into town, taking a longer route that
kept him well clear of the Portfield ranch, and disposed of his
eight gallons of *pulque* at Whalley's Saloon. The heat was intense,
and perspiration had glued his shirt to his back, but he allowed
himself only one glass of beer before going to see Ruth Jefferson in
her cousin's store. He found her alone at the rear of the store,

struggling to lift a sack of beans onto a low shelf. She was a sturdy, attractive woman in her early forties, still straight-backed and narrow-waisted even though ten years of widowhood and self-sufficiency had scored deep lines at the sides of her mouth.

"Afternoon, Billy," she said on hearing his footsteps, then looked at him more closely. "What are you up to, Billy Gregg?"

Gregg felt his heart falter—this was precisely the sort of thing that had always made him wary of women. "What do you mean?"

"I mean why are you wearing a necktie on a day like that? And your good hat? And, if I'm not mistaken, your good boots?"

"Let me help you with that sack," he said, going forward.

"It's too much for those arms of yours."

"I can manage." Gregg stooped, put his chest close to the sack, and gripped it between his upper arms. He straightened up, holding the sack awkwardly but securely, and dropped it onto the shelf. "See? What did I tell you?"

"You've got dust all over yourself," she said severely, flicking at his clothing with her handkerchief.

"It doesn't matter. Don't fuss." In spite of his protests, Gregg stood obediently and allowed himself to be dusted off, enjoying the attention. "I need your help, Ruth," he said, making a decision.

She nodded. "I've been telling you that for years."

"This is for one special thing, and I can't even tell you about it unless you promise to keep it secret."

"I knew it! I knew you were up to something as soon as you walked in here."

Gregg extracted the promise he wanted, then went on to describe the events of the morning. As he talked, the lines at the sides of Ruth's mouth grew more pronounced, and her eyes developed a hard, uncompromising glitter. He was relieved when, just as he had finished speaking, two women came into the store and spent ten minutes buying a length of cloth. By the time Ruth had finished serving them the set look had gone from her face, but he could tell she was still angry with him.

"I don't understand you, Billy," she whispered. "I thought you had learned your lesson the last time you went up against the Portfield crowd."

"There was nothing else I could do," he said. "I had to help her."

"That's what I'm afraid of."

"What does that mean?"

"Billy Gregg, if I ever find out that you got some little saloon girl into trouble and then had the nerve to get me to help with the delivery . . ."

"Ruth!" Gregg was genuinely shocked by the new idea.

"It's a more likely story than the one you've just told me."

He sighed and took the slim gold bar from his pocket. "Would she be paying me? With this sort of thing?"

"I suppose not," Ruth said. "But it's all so . . . What kind of a name is Morna?"

"Don't ask me."

"Well, where is she from?"

"Don't ask me."

"You've had a shave, as well." She stared at him in perplexity for a moment. "I guess I'll just have to go out there and meet the woman who can make Billy Gregg start prettying himself up. I want to see what she's got that I haven't."

"Thanks, Ruth—I feel a lot easier in my mind now." Gregg looked around the big shady room with its loaded shelves and beams festooned with goods. "What sort of stuff should I be taking back with me?"

"I'll make up a bundle of everything that's needed and take it out to you before supper. I can borrow Sam's gig."

"That's great." Gregg smiled his gratitude. "Make sure you use the west road, though."

"Get out of here and let me get on with my chores," Ruth said briskly. "None of Portfield's saddle tramps are going to bother me."

"Right—see you later." Gregg was turning to leave when his attention was caught by the bolts of cloth stacked on the counter. He fingered a piece of silky material and frowned. "Ruth, did you ever hear of cloth that looks silver out of doors and turns blue indoors?"

"No, I never did."

"I thought not." Gregg walked to the door, hesitated, then went out into the heat and throbbing brilliance of Copper Cross's main street. He got onto his buckboard, flicked the reins, and drove slowly to the water trough, which was in an alley at the side of the livery stables. A young cowboy with a drooping, sandy mustache was already watering his horse. Gregg recognized him as Cal Masham, one of the passably honest hands who worked for Josh Portfield, and nodded a greeting.

"Billy." Masham nodded in return and took his pipe from his mouth. "Heard about your run-in with Wolf Caley this forenoon."

"News gets around fast."

Masham glanced up and down the alley. "I think you ought to know, Billy—Wolf's hurt real bad."

"Yeah, I heard his leg go when his horse came down on it. I owed him a broken bone or two." Gregg sniffed appreciatively. "Nice tobacco you've got in there."

"It wasn't a clean break, Billy. Last I heard his leg was all swole up and turned black. And he's got a fever."

In the heat of the afternoon Gregg suddenly felt cool. "Is he likely to die?"

"It looks that way, Billy." Masham looked around him again. "Don't tell anybody I told you, but Josh is due back in two or three days. If I was in your shoes I wouldn't hang around and wait for him to get here."

"Thanks for the tip, son." Gregg waited impassively until his horse had finished drinking, then he urged the animal forward. It lowered its head and drew him from the shadow of the stables into the searing arena of the street.

Gregg had left the woman, Morna, sleeping on his bed and still wrapped in the flowing outer garment whose properties were such a mystery to him. On his return he entered the house quietly, hoping to avoid disturbing her rest, and found Morna sitting at the table with a book spread out before her. She had removed her cloak to reveal a simple blue smock with half-length sleeves. The book was one of the dozen that Gregg owned, a well-worn school atlas, and it was open at a double-page map of North America.

Morna had tied her fair hair into a loose coil, and she looked more beautiful than Gregg had remembered, but his attention was drawn to the strange ornament on her wrist. It looked like a circular piece of dark red glass about the size of a dollar, rimmed with gold and held in place by a thin gold band. Its design was unusual enough, but the thing that held Gregg's gaze was that under the surface of the glass was a sliver of ruby light, equivalent in size and positioning to one hand of a watch, which blinked on and off at intervals of about two seconds.

She looked up at him and smiled. "I hope you don't mind." She indicated the atlas.

"Help yourself, ma'am."

"Morna."

"Help yourself . . . Morna." The familiarity did not sit easily with Gregg. "Are you feeling stronger?"

"I'm much better, thank you. I hadn't slept since . . . for quite a long time."

"I see." Gregg sat down at the other side of the table and allowed himself a closer look at the intriguing ornament. On its outer rim were faint markings like those of a compass, and the splinter of light continued its slow pulsing beneath the glass. "I don't mean to pry, ma'am—Morna," he said, "but in my whole life I've never seen anything like that thing on your wrist."

"It's nothing." Morna covered it with her hand. "It's just a trinket."

"But how can it keep sparking the way it does?"

"Oh, I don't understand these matters," she said airily. "I believe it works by electronics."

"Is that something to do with electricity?"

"Electricity is what I meant to say—my English is not very good."

"But what's it *for?*"

Morna laughed. "Do your women only wear what is useful?"

"I guess not," Gregg said doubtfully, aware he was being put off once again. After a few initial uncertainties, Morna's English had been very assured, and he suspected that the odd word she had used—electronics—had not been a mistake. He made up his mind to search for it in Ruth's dictionary, if he ever got the chance.

Morna looked down at the atlas, upon which she had placed a piece of straw running east to west, with one end at the approximate location of Copper Cross. "According to this map we are about twelve hundred miles from New Orleans."

Gregg shook his head. "It's more than that to New Orleans."

"I've just measured it."

"That's the straight-line distance," he explained patiently. "It doesn't signify anything—'less you can fly like a bird."

"But you agree that it is twelve hundred miles."

"That's about right—for a bird." Gregg jumped to his feet and, in his irritation, tried to do it in the normal way, with the assistance of his arms pushing against the table. His left elbow cracked loudly and gave way, bringing him down on that shoulder. Embarrassed, he stood up more slowly, trying not to show that he was hurt, and walked to the range. "We'll have to see about getting you some proper food."

"What's wrong with your arm?" Morna spoke softly, from close behind him.

"It's nothing for you to worry about," he said, surprised at her show of concern.

"Let me see it, Billy—I may be able to help."

"You're not a doctor, are you?" As he had expected, there was no reply to his question, but the possibility that the woman had medical training prompted Gregg to roll up his sleeves and let her examine the misshapen elbow joints. Having unbent that far, he went on to tell her about how—in the absence of any law enforcement in the area—he had been foolish enough to let himself be talked into taking the job of unofficial town warden, and about how, even more foolishly, he had once interrupted Josh Portfield and four of his men in the middle of a drinking spree. He skimmed briefly over the details of how two men had held each of his wrists and whipped him bodily to and fro for over fifteen minutes until his elbows had snapped backward.

"Why is it always so?" she breathed.

"What was that, ma'am?"

Morna raised her eyes. "There's nothing I can do, Billy. The joints were fractured and now they have sclerosed over."

"Sclerosed, eh?" Gregg noted another word to be checked later.

"Do you get much pain?" She looked at the expression on his face. "That was a silly question, wasn't it?"

"It's a good thing I'm partial to whisky," he confessed. "Otherwise I wouldn't get much sleep some nights."

She smiled compassionately. "I think I can do something about the pain. It's in my own interest to get you as fit as possible by . . . What day is this?"

"Friday."

"By Sunday."

"Don't trouble yourself about Sunday," he said. "I've got a friend coming to help out. A woman friend," he added, as Morna stepped back from him, the hunted expression returning to her face.

"You promised not to tell anyone I was here."

"I know, but it's purely for your benefit. Ruth Jefferson is a fine lady, and I know her as well as I know myself. She won't talk to a living soul."

Morna's face relaxed slightly. "Is she important to you?"

"We were supposed to get married."

"In that case I won't object," Morna said, her gray eyes unreadable. "But please remember it was your own decision to tell her about me."

Ruth Jefferson came into sight about an hour before sunset, driving her cousin's gig.

Gregg, who had been watching for her, went into the house and tapped the open door of the bedroom, where Morna had lain down to rest without undressing. She awoke instantly with a startled gasp, glancing at the gold bracelet on her wrist. From his viewpoint in the doorway, Gregg noted that the ornament's imprisoned splinter of light seemed always to point to the east, and he decided it could be a strange form of compass. It might have been his imagination, but he had an impression that the light's rate of pulsation had increased slightly since he had first observed it in the morning. More wonderful and strange, however, was the overall sight of the golden-haired young woman, heavy with new life, who had come to him from out of nowhere, and whose very presence seemed to shed a glow over the plain furniture of his bedroom. He found himself speculating anew about the circumstances that had stranded such a creature in the near wilderness of his part of the world.

"Ruth will be here in a minute," he said. "Would you like to come out and meet her?"

"Very much." Morna smiled as she stood up and walked to the door with him. Gregg was slightly taken aback that she did so without touching her hair or fussing about her dress—in his experience first meetings between women usually were edgy occasions. Then he noticed that her simple hairstyle was undisturbed, and that the material of the blue smock, in spite of having been lain on for several hours, was as sleek and as smooth as if it had just come off the hanger. It was yet another addition to the dossier of curious facts he was assembling about his guest.

"Hello, Ruth—glad you could come." Gregg went forward to steady the gig and help Ruth down from it.

"I'll bet you are," Ruth said. "Have you heard about Wolf Caley?"

Gregg lowered his voice. "I heard he was fixing to die."

"That's right. What are you going to do about it?"

"What can I do?"

"You could head north as soon as it gets dark and keep going. I'm crazy to suggest it, but I could stay here and look after your lady friend."

"That wouldn't be fair." Gregg shook his head slowly. "No, I'm staying on here, where I'm needed."

"Just what do you think you'll be able to do when Josh Portfield and his mob come for you?"

"Ruth," he whispered uneasily, "I wish you'd talk about something else—you're going to upset Morna. Now come and meet her."

Ruth gave him an exasperated look, but went quietly with him to the house, where he performed the introductions. The women shook hands in silence, and then—quite spontaneously—both began to smile, the roles of mother and daughter tacitly assigned and mutually accepted. Gregg knew that communication had taken place on a level he would never understand, and his ingrained awe of the female mind increased.

He was pleased to see that Ruth, who had obviously been prepared to have her worst suspicions confirmed, was impressed with Morna. It would make his own life a little easier. While the two women went indoors he unloaded the supplies Ruth had brought, gripping the wicker basket between his upper arms to avoid stressing his elbows. When he carried it into the house and set it on the table, Ruth and Morna were deep in conversation, and Ruth broke off long enough to point at the door, silently commanding him to leave again.

Even more gratified, Gregg lifted a pack of tailor-mades from a shelf and went out to the shack, where his *pulque* still was in operation. He preferred hand-rolled cigarettes, but was accustomed to doing without them now that his fingers were incapable of the fine control required in the rolling of tobacco. Making himself comfortable on a stool in the corner, he lit a cigarette and contentedly surveyed his little domain of copper cooling coils, retorts, and tubs of fermenting cactus pulp. The knowledge that there were two women in his house, and that one of them was soon to have a child there, gave him a warm sense of importance he had never known before. He spent some time indulging himself in dreams, projected on screens of aromatic smoke, in which Ruth was his wife, Morna was his daughter, and he was again fit enough to do a real day's work and provide for his family.

"I don't know how you can sit in this place." Ruth was standing in the doorway, with a shawl around her shoulders. "That smell can't be healthy."

"It never did anybody any harm," Gregg said, rising to his feet. "Fermentation is part of nature."

"So is cow dung." Ruth backed out of the shack and waited for him to join her. In the reddish, horizontal light of the setting sun she looked healthy and attractive, imbued with a mature competence. "I have to go back now," she said, "but I'll be here again tomorrow, in the morning, and I'm going to stay until that baby is safely delivered into this world."

"I thought Saturday was your busy day at the store."

"It is, but Sam will have to manage on his own. I can't leave that child to have the baby by herself. You'd be worse than useless to her."

"But what's Sam going to think?"

"It doesn't matter what Sam thinks—I'll tell him you're poorly." Ruth paused for a moment. "Where do you think she's from, Billy?"

"Couldn't rightly say. She talked some about New Orleans."

Ruth frowned in disagreement. "Her talk doesn't sound like Louisiana talk to me—and she's got some real foreign notions to go with it."

"I noticed," Gregg said emphatically.

"The way she only talks about having a son? Just won't entertain the idea that it's just as likely to be a girl."

"Mmm." Gregg had been thinking about muzzle velocities of revolvers. "I wish I knew what she's running away from."

Ruth's features softened unexpectedly. "I've read lots of stories about women from noble families . . . heiresses and such . . . not allowed to acknowledge their own babies because the fathers were commoners."

"Ruth Jefferson," Gregg said gleefully, "I didn't know you were going around that homely old store with your head stuffed full of romantic notions."

"I do nothing of the sort." Ruth's color deepened. "But it's as plain as the nose on your face that Morna comes from money—and it's probably her own folks she's in trouble with."

"Could be." Gregg remembered the abject terror he had seen in Morna's eyes. His instincts told him she had more on her mind than outraged parents, but he decided not to argue with Ruth. He stood and listened patiently while she explained that she had put Morna to bed, about his own sleeping arrangements in the other room, and about the type of breakfast he was to prepare in the morning.

"And you leave the whisky jar alone tonight," Ruth concluded. "I don't want you lying around in a drunken stupor if that child's pains start during the night. You hear me?"

"I hear you—I wasn't planning to do any drinking, anyway. Do you think the baby will arrive on Sunday, like Morna says?"

Ruth seated herself in the gig and gathered up the traces. "Somehow—I don't know why—I'm inclined to believe it will. See you, Billy."

"Thanks, Ruth." Gregg watched until the gig had passed out of sight beyond a rocky spur of the hillside upon which his house was built, then he turned and went indoors. The door of the bedroom was closed. He made up a bed on the floor with the blankets Ruth had left out for him, but knew he was unready for sleep. Chuckling a little with guilty pleasure, he poured himself a generous measure of corn whisky from the stone jar he kept in the cupboard and settled down with it in his most comfortable chair. The embers of the sunset filled the room with mellow light, and as he sipped the companionable liquor Gregg felt a sense of fulfillment in his role of watchdog.

He even allowed himself to hope that Morna would stay with him for longer than the six days she had planned.

Gregg awoke with a start at dawn to find himself still sitting in the chair, the empty cup clasped in his hand. He went to set the cup aside and almost groaned aloud as the flexing of his elbow produced a sensation akin to glass fragments crunching against a raw nerve. It must have been cool during the night, and his unprotected arms had stiffened up far more than usual. He stood up with difficulty, was dismayed to see that his shirt and pants were a mass of wrinkles, and it came to him that a man living alone should have clothes impervious to creases, clothes like those of . . .

Morna!

As recollections of the previous day fountained in his head, Gregg hurried to the range and began cleaning it out in preparation for lighting a fire. Ruth had left instructions that he was to heat milk and oatmeal for Morna's breakfast, and provide her with a basin of warm water in her room. Partly because of his haste, and partly because of the difficulty of controlling his fingers, he dropped the fire irons several times and was hardly surprised to hear the bedroom door opening soon afterward. Morna appeared in the opening wearing a flowered dressing gown that Ruth must have brought for her. The familiar, feminine styling of the garment made her prettier in Gregg's eyes, and at the same time more approachable.

"Good morning," he said. "Sorry about all the noise. I hope I didn't . . ."

"I'd caught up on my sleep anyway." She came into the room, sat at the table, and placed on it a second of the slim gold bars. "This is for you, Billy."

He pushed it back toward her. "I don't want it. The one you gave me is worth more than anything I can do for you."

Morna gave him a calm, sad smile, and he was abruptly reminded that she was not a home-grown girl discussing payment for a domestic chore. "You risked your life for me—and I think you would do it again. Would you?"

Gregg looked away from her. "I didn't do much."

"But you did! I was watching you, Billy, and I saw that you were afraid—but I also saw that you were able to control the fear. It made you stronger instead of weaker, and that's something that even the finest of my people are unable . . ." Morna broke off and pressed the knuckles of one hand to her lips as though she had been on the verge of revealing a secret.

"We'll have something to eat soon." Gregg turned back toward the range. "As soon as I get a fire going."

"You haven't answered my question."

He shifted his feet. "What question?"

"If somebody came here to kill me—and to kill my son—would you defend us even if it meant placing your own life at risk?"

"This is just crazy," Gregg protested. "Why should anybody want to kill you?"

Her eyes locked fast on his. "Answer the question, Billy."

"I . . ." The words were as difficult for Gregg as a declaration of love. "Do I need to answer it? Do you think I would run away?"

"No," she said gently. "That's all the answer I need."

"I'm pleased about that." Gregg's voice was gruffer than he had meant it to be, because Morna—who was half his age—kept straying in his mind from the role of foster daughter to that of lover wife, in spite of the facts that he scarcely knew her and that she was swollen with another man's child. He was oppressed by the sinfulness of his thinking and by fears of making a fool of himself, yet he was deeply gratified by Morna's trust. No man, he decided, no prince, not even the Prince of Darkness himself, was going to harm or distress her if there was anything he could do to prevent it. While he busied himself with getting a fire going, Gregg made up his mind to check the condition of his Remington as soon as he could do so without being seen by Morna or Ruth. In the unlikely event that he might need it, he would also inspect the percussion caps and loads in the old Tranter he had taken from Wolf Caley.

As though divining the turn of his thoughts, Morna said, "Billy, have you a long gun? A rifle?"

He puffed out his cheeks. "Never owned one."

"Why not? The longer barrel would allow the charge to impart more energy to the bullet and give you a more effective weapon."

Gregg hunched his shoulders and refused to turn round, somehow offended at hearing Morna's light, clear voice using the terminology of the armorer. "Never wanted one," he said.

"But *why* not?"

"I was never all that good with a rifle, even when my arms were all right, so it's safer for me not to carry one. There's no law to speak of in these parts, you see. If a man uses a revolver to kill another man he generally gets off with it, provided the man he shot was carrying a wheel gun too. Even if he didn't get a chance to draw it, it's classed as a fair fight. The same goes if they both have rifles, but I'm none too good with a rifle—so I'm not going to risk having somebody I crossed knock me over at two hundred yards and claim it was self-defense." The speech was the longest Gregg had made in months, and he expressed his displeasure at having had to make it by raking the ashes in the fire basket with unnecessary vigor.

"I see," Morna said thoughtfully behind him. "A simple duello variation. Are you accurate with a revolver?"

For a reply Gregg started slamming the range's cooking rings back into place.

Her voice assumed the imperious quality he had heard in it before. "Billy, are you accurate with a revolver?"

He wheeled on her, holding out his arms in such a way as to display the misshapen, knotted elbows. "I can point a six-shooter just like I always could, but it takes me so long to get it up there I wouldn't be a match for a ten-year-old boy. Is that what you wanted to know?"

"There is no room for anger between us." Morna stood up and

took his outstretched hands in hers. She looked into his face with searching gray eyes. "You love me, don't you, Billy?"

"Yes." Gregg heard the word across a distance, knowing he could not have said it to a stranger.

"I'm proud that you do—now wait here." Morna went into the bedroom, took something from an inner part of her cloak, and returned with what at first seemed to be a small square of green glass. Gregg was surprised to see that it was as pliable as a piece of buckskin, and he watched with growing puzzlement as Morna pressed it to his left elbow. It was curiously warm against his skin, and a tingling sensation seemed to pass right through the joint.

"Bend your arm," Morna ordered, now as impersonal as an army surgeon.

Gregg did as he was told and was thrilled to find there was no pain, no grinding of arthritic glass needles. He was still flexing his left arm, speechless with disbelief, when Morna repeated the procedure with his right, achieving the same miraculous result. For the first time in two years, Gregg could bend his arms freely and without suffering in the process.

Morna smiled up at him. "How do they feel?"

"Like new—just like new."

"They'll never be as good or as strong as they were," Morna said, "but I can promise you there'll be no more pain." She went back into the bedroom and emerged a moment later without the transparent green square. "Now, I think you said something about food."

Gregg shook his head. "There's something going on here. You're not who you claim to be. Nobody can do the sort of . . ."

"I didn't claim to be anybody," Morna said quite sharply, with yet another of her swift changes of mood.

"Perhaps I should have said you're not *what* you claim to be."

"Don't spoil things, Billy . . . I have nobody but you." Morna sat down at the table and covered her face with her hands.

"I'm sorry." Gregg was reaching out to touch her when, for the first time that morning, he noticed the curious gold ornament on her wrist. The imprisoned splinter of light was pointing east as usual, but it was brighter than it had been yesterday and was definitely flashing at a higher rate. Gregg, becoming attuned to strangeness, was unable to avoid the impression that it was pulsing out some kind of warning.

True to her word, Ruth arrived early in the day.

She had brought extra supplies, including a jug of broth, which was wrapped in a traveling rug to retain its warmth. Gregg was glad to see her and grateful for the womanly efficiency with which she took control of his household, yet he was discomfited at finding himself made redundant. He spent more and more time in the shack, tending to his stills, and that bright moment in which there had been talk of love between Morna and him began to seem like a figment of his imagination. He was not deluding himself that she had referred to husband-and-wife love, perhaps not father-and-daughter love either, but the mere use of the word had, for a brief span, made his life less sterile, and he treasured it.

Ruth, in contrast, spoke of commodity prices and scarcities, dress-making and local affairs—and, in the aura of normalcy that surrounded her, Gregg decided against mentioning the fantastic cure that Morna had wrought on his arms. He had a feeling she would refuse to believe, and—by robbing him of his faith—neutralize the magic or unwork the miracle. Ruth came to visit him in the shack in the afternoon, covering her nose with her handkerchief, but it was only to tell him privately that Wolf Caley was not expected to last out the day, and that Josh Portfield and his men were reported to be riding north from Sonora.

Gregg thanked her for the information and gave no sign of being affected by it, but at the first opportunity he smuggled his Remington and Caley's Tranter out of the house and devoted some time to ensuring that they were in serviceable condition.

Portfield had always been an enigmatic figure in Gregg's life. The big spread he owned had been passed on to him by his father, and it was profitable; therefore there was no need for Josh to engage in unlawful activities. He had, however, acquired a taste for violence during the war, and the troubled territories of Mexico lying only a short distance to the south seemed to draw him like a magnet. Every now and then he would take a bunch of men and go on a kind of motiveless unofficial "raid" beyond the border. Portfield was far from being a mad dog, often leading a fairly normal existence for months on end, but he appeared to lack any conception of right and wrong.

For example, he genuinely believed he had been lenient with Gregg by merely ruining his arms, instead of killing him, for interrupting that fateful drinking spree. Afterward, on meeting Gregg on the trail or in Copper Cross, he had always hailed him in the friendliest manner possible, apparently under the impression he had earned Gregg's gratitude and respect. Each man, Gregg had discovered, lives in his own reality.

There was always the possibility that, when Portfield learned of Caley's misfortune, he would shrug and say that any man who worked for him ought to be able to cope with an aging cripple. Gregg had known Portfield to make equally unexpected judgments, but he had a suspicion that on this occasion the hammer of Portfield's anger was going to come down hard and that he was going to be squarely underneath it. In a way he could not understand, his apprehension was fed and magnified by Morna's own mysterious fears.

During the meals, while the three of them were seated at the rough wooden table, he was content to have Ruth carry the burden of conversation with Morna. The talk was mainly of domestic matters, on any of which Morna might have been drawn out to reveal something of her own background, but she skirted Ruth's various traps with easy diplomacy.

Late in the evening Morna began to experience the first contraction pains, and from that point Gregg found himself relegated by Ruth to the status of an inconvenient piece of furniture. He accepted the treatment without rancor, having been long familiar with the subdued hostility that women feel toward men during a confinement, and willingly performed every task given to him. Only an occasional brooding glance from Morna reminded him that between them was a covenant of which Ruth, for all her matronly competence, knew nothing.

The baby was born at noon on Sunday, and—as Morna had predicted—it was a boy.

"Don't let Morna do too much," Ruth said on Monday morn-

ing, as she seated herself in the gig. "She has no business being up
and about so soon after a birth."

Gregg nodded. "Don't worry—I'll take care of all the chores."

"Do that." Ruth looked at him with sudden interest. "How are
your arms these days?"

"Better. They feel a lot easier."

"That's good." Ruth picked up the reins but seemed reluctant
to drive away. Her gaze strayed toward the house, where Morna
was standing with the baby cradled in her arms. "I suppose you
can't wait for me to go and leave you alone with your ready-made
family."

"Now, you know that's not right, Ruth. You know how much I
appreciate all you've done here. You're not jealous, are you?"

"Jealous?" Ruth shook her head, then gave him a level stare.
"Morna is a strange girl. She's not like me, and she's not like you—
but I've got a feeling there's something going on between you
two."

Gregg's fear of Ruth's intuitive powers stirred anew. "You
know, Ruth, you're starting to sound like one of those new phono-
graphs."

"Oh, I don't mean hanky-panky," she said quickly, "but you're
up to something. I know you."

"I'll be in to settle up my bill in a day or two," Gregg parried.
"Soon as I can change one of those gold bars."

"Try to do it before Josh Portfield gets back." Ruth flicked the
reins and drove down the hillside.

Gregg took a deep breath and surveyed the distant blue ramparts of the sierras before walking back to the house. Morna was
still wearing the flowered dressing gown and, with the shawl-
wrapped baby in her arms, she looked much like any other young
mother. The single uncomformity in her appearance was the gold
ornament on her wrist. Even in the brightness of the morning sunlight, its needle of crimson light was harshly brilliant, and its pul-
sations had speeded up to several a second. Gregg had thought a
lot about the ornament during his spells of solitude over the previous two days, and he had convinced himself he understood its
function if not its nature. He felt that the time had come for some
plain talking.

Morna went indoors with him. The birth had been straightforward and easy for her, but her face was pale and drawn, and there was a tentative quality about the smile she gave him as he closed the door.

"It feels strange for us to be alone again," Morna said quietly.

"Very strange." Gregg pointed at the flashing bracelet. "But it looks as though we won't be alone for very long."

She sat down abruptly, and her baby raised one miniature pink hand in protest at the sudden movement. Morna drew the infant closer to her breast. She lowered her face to the baby, touching its forehead with hers, and her hair fell forward, screening it with strands of gold.

"I'm sorry," Gregg said, "but I need to know who it is that's coming out of the east. I need to know who I'm going up against."

"I can't tell you that, Billy."

"I see—I'm entitled to get killed, maybe, but not to know who does it, or why."

"Please don't." Her voice was muffled. "Please understand . . . that I can't tell you anything."

Gregg felt a pang of guilt. He went to Morna and knelt beside her. "Why don't we both—the three of us, I mean—get out of here right now? We could load up my buckboard and be gone in ten minutes."

Morna shook her head without looking up. "It wouldn't make any difference."

"It would make a difference to me."

At that, Morna raised her head and looked at him with anxious, brimming eyes. "This man, Portfield—will he try to kill you?"

"Did Ruth tell you about him?" Gregg clicked his tongue with annoyance. "She shouldn't have done that. You've got enough to . . ."

"Will he try to kill you?"

Gregg was impelled to tell the unvarnished truth. "It isn't so much a matter of him *trying* to kill me, Morna. He rides around in company with seven or eight hard cases, and if they decide to kill somebody they just go right ahead and do it."

"Oh!" Morna seemed to regain something of her former resolve. "My son can't travel yet, but I'll get him ready as soon as I can. I'll try hard, Billy."

"That's fine with me," Gregg said uncertainly. He had an uneasy feeling that the conversation had gotten beyond him in some way, but he had lost the initiative and was in no way equipped to deal with a woman's tears.

"That's all right, then." He got to his feet and looked down at the baby's absurdly tiny features. "Have you thought of a name for the little fellow yet?"

Morna relaxed momentarily, looking pleased. "It's too soon. The naming time is still above him."

"In English," Gregg gently corrected, "we say that the future is ahead of us, not above us."

"But that implies linear . . ." Morna checked her words. "You're right, of course—I should have said ahead."

"My mother was a schoolmarm," he said inconsequentially, once more with an odd sense that communications between them were failing. "I've got some work to do outside, but I'll be close by if you need me."

Gregg went to the door, and as he was closing it behind him he looked back into the room. He saw that, yet again, Morna was sitting with her forehead pressed to that of her son, something he had never seen other women doing. He dismissed it as the least puzzling of her idiosyncracies. In fact, there was no pressing work to be done outside—but he had a gut feeling that the time had come for keeping an eye on all approaches to his house. He walked slowly to the top of the saddleback, threading his way among boulders that resembled grazing sheep, and settled down on the eastern crest. A careful scan with his telescope revealed no activity in the direction of the Portfield ranch or on the trail running south to Copper Cross. Gregg then pointed the little instrument due east toward where the Rio Grande flowed unseen between the northern extremities of the Sierra Madre and the Sacramento Mountains. Visibility was good, and his eye was dazzled with serried vistas of peaks and ranges on a scale too vast for comprehension.

You're letting yourself get spooked, he thought irritably. *Noth-*

ing crosses country in a straight line like a bird—except another bird.

He contrived to spend most of the day on the vantage point, though making frequent trips down to the house to check on Morna, to prepare two simple meals, and to boil water for washing the baby's diapers. It pleased him to note that the child slept almost continuously between feeds, thus giving Morna plenty of opportunity to rest. At times Ruth's phrase "ready-made family" came to his mind, and he realized how appropriate it had been. Even in the bizarre circumstances that prevailed, there was something deeply satisfying about having a woman and child under his roof, looking to him and to no other man for their welfare and safety. The relationship made him something more than he had been. Although he did his best to repress the thought, the possibility suggested itself that, were Morna and he to flee north together, she might never return to her former life. In that case, he might indeed acquire a ready-made family.

Gregg shied away from pursuing that line of thought too far.

Late in the evening, when the sun was dipping toward the lower ranges beyond far Mexicali, he saw a lone horseman approaching from the direction of the Portfield ranch. The rider was moving at a leisurely pace, and the fact that he was alone was an indication that there was no trouble afoot, but Gregg decided not to take any chances. He walked down the hill past the house, took the Remington from its hiding place in the shack, and went on down to take up his position on the spur of rock where the trail bent sharply. When the horseman came into view he was slumped casually in the saddle, obviously half asleep, and his hat was pulled down to screen his eyes from the low-slanted rays of the sun. Gregg recognized Cal Masham, the young cowboy he had spoken to in the town on Friday.

"What are you doing in these parts, Cal?" he shouted.

Masham jerked upright, his jaw sagging with shock. "Billy? You still here?"

"What does it look like?"

"Hell, I figured you'd be long gone by this time."

"And you wanted to see what I'd left behind—is that it?"

Masham grinned beneath the drooping mustache. "It seemed

to me you'd leave those big heavy crocks of *pulque,* and it seemed to me I might as well have them as somebody else. After all . . ."

"You can have a drink on me any time," Gregg said firmly, "but not tonight. You'd best be on your way, Cal."

Masham looked displeased. "Seems to me you're wavin' that gun at the wrong people, Billy. Did you know that Wolf Caley's dead?"

"I hadn't heard."

"Well, he is. And Big Josh'll be home tomorrow. Max Tibbett rode in ahead this afternoon, and as soon as he heard about Wolf he took a fresh horse and rode south again to tell Josh. You just shouldn't *be* here, Billy." Masham's voice had taken on a rising note of complaint, and he seemed genuinely upset by Gregg's fool-hardiness in remaining.

Gregg considered for a moment. "Come up and help yourself to a jar, but don't make any noise—I've got a guest and a newborn baby I don't want disturbed."

"Thanks, Billy." Masham dismounted and walked up the hill with Gregg. He accepted a heavy stone jar, glancing curiously toward the house, and rode off with his prize clasped to his chest.

Gregg watched him out of sight, put the Remington away, and decided that he was entitled to a shot of whisky to counter the effects of the news he had just received. He crossed the familiar ruts of the buckboard's turning circle and looked in through the front window of the house to see if Morna was in the main room. He had intended only to glance in quickly while passing the window, but the strange tableau within checked him in midstride.

Morna was dressed in her own blue maternity smock, which appeared to have been reshaped to her slimmer figure, although Gregg had not noticed her or Ruth doing any needlework. She had spread a white sheet over the table and her baby was lying in the center of it, naked except for the binder that crossed his navel. Morna was standing beside the table, with both hands clasping the baby's head. Her eyes were closed, lips moving silently, her face as cold and masklike as that of a high priestess performing an ancient ceremony.

Gregg desperately wanted to turn away, convinced he was guilty of an invasion of privacy, but a change was taking place in

Morna's appearance, and the slow progression of it induced a mesmeric paralysis of his limbs. As he watched, Morna's golden hair began to stir, as though it were some complex living creature in its own right. Her head was absolutely motionless, but gradually—over a period of about ten seconds—her hair fanned out, each strand becoming straight and seemingly rigid, to form a bright, fearsome halo. Gregg felt his mouth go dry as he witnessed Morna's dreadful transformation from the normalcy of young motherhood to the semblance of a witch figure. She bent forward from the waist until her forehead was touching that of the baby.

There was a moment of utter stillness—and then her body became transparent.

Gregg felt icy ripples move upward from the back of his neck into his own hair as he realized that he could see right through Morna. She was indisputably present in the room, yet the lines of walls and furniture continued on through her body, as if she were an image superimposed on them by a magic lantern.

The baby made random pawing movements with his arms and legs, but otherwise appeared to be unaffected by what was happening. Morna remained in the same state, somewhere between matter and mirage, for several seconds, then quite abruptly she was as solid as before. She straightened up, and Gregg could see that her hair was beginning to subside into its previous helmet shape of loose waves. She smoothed it down with her hands and turned toward the window.

Gregg lunged to one side in terror and scampered, doubled over like a man dodging gunfire, for the cover of his buckboard, which he had left on the blind side of the house. He crouched there, breathing noisily, until he was sure Morna had not seen him, then made his way to his customary spot at the top of the saddleback, where he squatted down and lit a cigarette. Even with the sane reassurance of tobacco, it was some time before his heart slowed to a steady rhythm. He was not a superstitious man, but his limited reading had taught him that there was a special kind of woman—known from biblical En-dor to the Salem of more recent times—who could work magical cures, and who often had to flee from persecution. One part of his mind rebelled against applying that name to a child like Morna, but there was no denying what he had just seen, no getting away from all the other strange things about her.

He smoked four more cigarettes, taking perhaps an hour to do so, then went back to his house. Morna—looking as normal and sweet and wholesome as a freshly baked apple pie—had lit an oil lantern and was brewing coffee. Her baby was peacefully asleep in the basket Ruth had left for it. Morna had even removed her gold bracelet, as though deliberately setting out to make him forget that she was in any way out of the ordinary. When Gregg glanced into the darkness of the bedroom, however, he saw the ruby glow, flashing so quickly now that its warning was almost continuous.

And it was far into the night before he finally managed to sleep.

Gregg was awakened in the morning by the thin, lonely bleat of the baby crying. He listened to it for what seemed a long time, expecting to hear Morna respond, but no other sound reached him from beyond the closed door of the bedroom. No matter what else she might be, Morna had impressed Gregg as a conscientious mother, and her prolonged inactivity at first puzzled and then began to worry him. He got up out of his bedroll, pulled on his pants, and tapped the door. There was no reply, apart from the baby's cries, which were as regular as breathing. He tapped again, more loudly, and pushed the door open.

The baby was in its basket beside the bed—Gregg could see the movement of tiny fists—but Morna had gone.

Unable to accept the evidence of his eyes, Gregg walked all around the square room and even looked below the bed. Morna's clothes, including her cloak, were missing too, and the only conclusion Gregg could reach was that she had risen during the hours of darkness, dressed herself, and left the house. To do so she would have had to pass within a few feet of where he was sleeping on the floor of the main room without disturbing him, and he was positive that nobody, not the most practiced thief, not the most skillful Indian tracker, could have done that. But then—the slow stains of memory began to spread in his mind—he was thinking in terms of normal human beings, and he had proof that Morna was far from normal.

The baby went on crying, its eyes squeezed shut, protesting in the only way it knew how about the absence of food and maternal warmth. Gregg stared at it helplessly, and it occurred to him that Morna might have left for good, making the infant his permanent responsibility.

"Hold on there, little fellow," he said, recalling that he had not checked outside the house. He left the bedroom, went outside, and called Morna's name. His voice faded into the air, absorbed by the emptiness of the morning landscape, and his horse looked up in momentary surprise from its steady cropping of the grass near the water pump. Gregg made a hurried inspection of his two outbuildings—the distilling shack and the ramshackle sentry box that was his lavatory—then decided he would have to take the baby into town and hand it over to Ruth. He had no idea how long a child of that age could survive without food, and he did not want to take unnecessary risks. Swearing under his breath, he turned back to the house and froze as he saw a flash of silver on the trail at the bottom of the hill.

Morna had just come around the spur of rock and was walking toward him. She was draped in her ubiquitous cloak, which had returned to its original color, and was carrying a small blue sack in one hand. Gregg's relief at seeing her pushed aside all his fears and reservations of the previous night, and he ran down the slope to meet her.

"Where have you been?" he called, while they were still some distance apart. "What was the idea of running off like that?"

"I didn't run off, Billy." She gave him a tired smile. "There were things I had to do."

"What sort of things? The baby's crying for a feed."

Morna's perfect young face was strangely hard. "What's a little hunger?"

"That's a funny way to talk," Gregg said, taken aback.

"The future simply doesn't exist for you, does it?" Morna looked at him with what seemed to be a mixture of pity and anger. "Don't you ever think ahead? Have you forgotten that we have . . . enemies?"

"I take things as they come. It's all a man can do."

Morna thrust the blue sack at him. "Take this as it comes."

"What is it?" Gregg accepted the bag and was immediately

struck by the fact that it was not made of blue paper, as he had supposed. The material was thin, strong, smooth to the touch, more pliable than oilskin, and without oilskin's underlying texture. "What is this stuff?"

"It's a new waterproof material," Morna said impatiently. "The contents are more important."

Gregg opened the sack and took out a large black revolver. It was much lighter than he would have expected for its size, and it had something of the familiar lines of a Colt except that the grips were grooved for individual fingers and flared out at the top over his thumb. Gregg had never felt a gun settle itself in his hand so smoothly. He examined the weapon more closely and saw that it had a six-shot fluted cylinder that hinged out sideways for easy loading—a feature he had never seen on any other firearm. The gun lacked any kind of decoration, but was more perfectly machined and finished than he could have imagined possible. He read the engraving on the side of the long barrel.

"Colt .44 Magnum," he said slowly. "Never heard of it. Where did you get this gun, Morna?"

She hesitated. "I've been up for hours. I left this near the road where you first saw me, and I had time to go back for it."

The story did not ring true to Gregg, but his mind was fully occupied by the revolver itself. "I mean, where did you get it *before?* Where can you buy a gun like this?"

"That doesn't matter." Morna began walking toward the house. "The point is: Could you use it?"

"I guess so," Gregg said, glancing into the blue bag, which still contained a cardboard box of brass cartridges. The top of the box was missing, and many of the shells had fallen into the bottom of the bag. "It's a right handsome gun, but I doubt if it packs any more punch than my Remington."

"I would like you to try it out." Morna was walking so quickly that Gregg had difficulty in keeping up with her. "Please see if you can load it."

"You mean right now? Don't you want to see to the baby?" They had reached the flat area in front of the house, and the child's cries had become audible.

Morna glanced at her wrist, and he saw that the gold ornament was burning with a steady crimson light. "My son can wait a while longer," she said in a voice that was firm and yet edged with panic. "Please load the revolver."

"Whatever you say." Gregg walked to his buckboard and used it as a table. He cleared a space in the straw, set the gun down, and—under Morna's watchful gaze—carefully spilled the ammunition out of the blue bag. The center-fire shells were rather longer than he had ever seen for a handgun and, like the revolver itself, were finished with a degree of perfection he had never encountered previously. Their noses shone like polished steel.

"Everything's getting too fancy—adds to the price," Gregg muttered. He fumbled with the weapon until he saw how to swing the cylinder out, then slipped in six cartridges and closed it up. As he was doing so he noticed that the cardboard box had emerged from the bag upside down, and on its underside, stamped in pale blue ink, he saw a brief inscription: "OCT 1978." He picked it up and held it out to Morna.

"Wonder what that means."

Her eyes widened slightly, then she looked away without interest. "It's just a maker's code. A batch number."

"It looks like a date," Gregg commented, "except that they've made a mistake and put . . ." He broke off, startled, as Morna knocked the box from his hands.

"Get on with it, you fool," she shouted, trampling the box underfoot. Her pale features were distorted with anger as she stared up at him with white-flaring eyes. They confronted each other for a moment, then her lips began to tremble. "I'm sorry, Billy. I'm so sorry . . . it's just that there's almost no time above us . . . and I'm afraid."

"It's all right," he said awkwardly. "I know I've got aggravating ways—Ruth's always telling me that—and I've been living alone for so long . . ."

Morna stopped him by placing a hand on his wrist. "Don't, Billy. You're a good and kind man, but I want you—right now, please—to learn to handle that gun." Her quiet, controlled tones somehow gave Gregg a greater sense of urgency than anything said previously.

"Right." He turned away from the buckboard, looking for a

suitable target, and began to ease the revolver's hammer back with his thumb.

"You don't need to do that," Morna said. "For rapid fire you just pull the trigger."

"I know—double action." Gregg cocked the gun regardless, to demonstrate his superior knowledge of firearms practice, and for a target selected a billet of wood that was leaning against the heavy stone water trough about twenty paces away. He was lining the gun's sights on it when Morna spoke again.

"You should hold it with both hands."

Gregg smiled indulgently. "Morna, you're a very well-educated young lady, and I daresay you know all manner of things I never even heard of—but don't try to teach an old hand like me how to shoot a six-gun." He steadied the gun, held his breath, and squeezed off his first shot. There was an explosion like a clap of thunder, and something struck him a fierce blow on the forehead, blinding him with pain. His first confused thought was that the revolver had been faulty and had burst open, throwing a fragment into his face. Then he found it was intact in his hand, and it dawned on him that there had been a massive recoil, which had bent his weakened arm like a piece of straw, swinging the weapon all the way back to collide with his forehead. He wiped a warm trickle of blood away from his eyes and looked at the gun with awe and the beginnings of a great respect.

"There isn't any smoke," he said. "There isn't even . . ."

His speech faltered as he looked beyond the gun in his hand and saw that the stone water trough, which had served as a backing for his target, had been utterly destroyed. Fragments of three-inch-thick earthenware were scattered over a triangular area running back about thirty yards. Without previous knowledge, Gregg would have guessed that the trough had been demolished by a cannon shot.

Morna took her hands away from her ears. "You've hurt yourself—I told you to hold it with both hands."

"I'm all right." He fended off her attempt to touch his forehead. "Morna, where did you get this . . . this *engine?*"

"Do you expect me to answer that?"

"I guess not, but I sure would like to know. This is something I could understand."

"Try it at longer range, and use both hands this time." Morna looked about her, apparently more composed now that Gregg was doing what she expected of him. She pointed at a whitish rock about three hundred yards off along the hillside. "That rock."

"That's getting beyond rifle range," Gregg explained. "Handguns don't . . ."

"Try it, Billy."

"All right—I'll try aiming way above it."

"Aim onto it, near the top."

Gregg shrugged and did as he was told, suddenly aware that his right thumb was throbbing painfully where the big revolver had driven back against it. He squeezed off his second shot and experienced a deep pang of satisfaction, of a kind that only hunters understand, when he saw dust fountain into the air only about a yard to the right of the rock. Even with his two-handed grip the gun had kicked back until it was pointing almost vertically into the sky. Without waiting to be told, he fired again and saw rock fragments fly from his target.

Morna nodded her approval. "You appear to have a talent."

"This is the best gun I ever saw," he told her sincerely, "but I can't hold it down. These arms of mine can't handle the recoil."

"Then we'll bind your elbows."

"Too late for that," he said regretfully, pointing down the slope.

Several horsemen were coming into view, their presence in the formerly deserted landscape more shocking to Gregg than the discovery of a scorpion in a picnic hamper.

He began cursing his own carelessness in not having kept a lookout as more riders emerged from beyond the spur until there were eight of them fanning out across the bottom of the hill. They were a mixed bunch, slouching or riding high according to individual preference, on mounts that varied from quarter horses to tall stallions, and their dress ranged from greasy buckskin to gambler's black. Gregg knew, however, that they constituted a miniature army, disciplined and controlled by one man. He narrowed his eyes against the morning brilliance and picked out the distinctive figure of Josh Portfield on a chestnut stallion. As always, Portfield was wearing a white shirt and a suit of charcoal gray serge, which might have given him the look of a preacher had it not been for the pair of nickel-plated Smith & Wessons strapped to his waist.

"I was kind of hoping Big Josh would leave things as they were," Gregg said. "He must be in one of his righteous moods."

Morna took an involuntary step backward. "Can you defend yourself against so many?"

"Have to give it a try." Gregg began scooping up handfuls of cartridges and cramming them into his pockets. "You'd best get inside the house and bar the door."

Morna looked up at him, the hunted look returning to her face, then she stooped to pick up something from the ground and ran to the house. Glancing sideways, Gregg was unable to understand why she should have wasted time retrieving the flattened cartridge box, but he had more important things on his mind. He flipped the revolver's cylinder out, dropped the three empty cases, and replaced them with new shells. Feeling sad rather than afraid, he walked a few paces toward the advancing riders. They had closed to within two hundred yards.

"Stay off my land, Josh," he shouted. "There's a law against trespassing."

Portfield stood up in his stirrups, and his powerful voice came clearly to Gregg in spite of the distance. "You're insolent, Billy. And you're ungrateful. And you've cost me a good man. I'm going to punish you for all those things, but most of all I'm going to punish you for your insolence and lack of respect." He sank down in the saddle and said something Gregg could not hear. A second later Siggy Sorenson urged his horse ahead of the pack and came riding up the hill with a pistol in his hand.

"This time I got a gun, too," Sorenson shouted. "This time we fight fair, eh?"

"If you come any farther I'll drop you," Gregg warned.

Sorenson began to laugh. "You're way out of range, you old fool. Can't you see any more?" He spurred his horse into a full gallop, and at the same time two other men went off to Gregg's left.

Gregg raised the big revolver and started to calculate bullet drop, then remembered it was practically nonexistent with the unholy weapon that fate had placed in his hands. This time the two-handed, knees-bent stance came to him naturally. He lined up on Sorenson, let him come on for another few seconds, and then squeezed the trigger. Sorenson's massive body, blasted right out of the saddle, turned over backward in midair and landed face down on the stony ground. His horse wheeled to one side and bolted. Realizing he would soon lose the advantage of surprise, Gregg turned on the two riders who were flanking him to the left. His second shot flicked the nearest man to the ground, and the third—fired too quickly—killed the other's horse. The animal dropped instantaneously, without a sound, and its rider threw himself into the shelter of its body, dragging a red-glinting leg.

Gregg looked back down the trail and in that moment discovered the quality of his opposition. He could see a knot of milling horses, but no men. In the brief respite given to them they had faded from sight behind rocks, no doubt with rifles taken from their saddle holsters. Suddenly becoming aware of how vulnerable he was in his exposed position at the top of the rise, Gregg bent low and ran for the cover of his shack. Crouching down behind it, he again dropped three expended cartridges and replaced them, appreciative of the speed with which the big gun could be loaded. He peered around a corner of the shack to make certain that nobody was working closer to him.

Shockingly, a pistol thundered, and black smoke billowed only twenty yards away. Something gouged through his lower ribs. Gregg lurched back into cover and stared in disbelief at the ragged and bloody tear in his shirt. He had been within a handsbreadth of death.

"You're too slow, Mr. Gregg," a voice called, frighteningly close at hand. "That old buffalo gun you got yourself don't make no difference if you're too slow."

Gregg identified the speaker as Frenchy Martine, a young savage from the Canadian backwoods who had drifted into Copper Cross a year earlier. The near-fatal shot had come from the direction of the upright coffin that was Gregg's primitive lavatory. Gregg had no idea how Martine had gotten that close in the time available, and it came home to him that a man of fifty was out of his class when it came to standing off youngsters in their prime.

"Tell you something else, Mr. Gregg," Martine chuckled. "You're too old for that choice piece of woman flesh you got tucked away in your . . ."

Gregg took one step to the side and fired at the narrow structure, punching a hole through the one-inch timbers as if they had been paper. There was the sound of a body hitting the ground beyond it, and a pistol tumbled into view. Gregg stepped back into the lee of the shack just as a rifle cracked in the distance, and he heard the impact as the slug buried itself in the wood. He drew slight comfort from the knowledge that his opponents were armed with ordinary weapons—because the real battle was now about to begin.

Martine had assumed he was safe behind two thicknesses of timber, but there were at least four others who would not make the same fatal mistake. Their most likely tactic would be to surround Gregg, keeping in the shelter of rock all the way, and then nail him down with long-range rifle fire. Gregg failed to see how, even with the black engine of death in his hands, he was going to survive the next hour, especially as he was losing quantities of blood.

He knelt down, made a rectangular pad with his handkerchief, and tucked it into his shirt in an attempt to slow the bleeding. Nobody was firing at him for the minute, so he took advantage of the lull to discard the single empty shell and make up the full load again. A deceptive quietness had descended over the area.

He looked around him at the sunlit hillside, with its rocks like grazing sheep, and tried to guess where the next shot might come from. His view of his surroundings blurred slightly, and there followed the numb realization that he might know nothing about the next shot until it was sledging its way through his body. A throbbing hum began to fill his ears—familiar prelude to the loss of consciousness—and he looked across the open, dangerous space that separated him from the house, wondering if he could get that far without being hit again. The chances were not good, but if he could get inside the house he might have time to bind his chest properly.

Gregg stood up and then became aware of the curious fact that, although the humming sound had grown much louder, he was relatively clear-headed. It was dawning on him that the powerful sound, like the swarming of innumerable hornets, had an objective reality, when he heard a man's deep-chested bellow of fear, followed by a fusillade of shots. He flinched instinctively, but there were no sounds of bullet strikes close by. Gregg risked a look down the sloping trail, and what he saw caused an icy prickling on his forehead.

A tall, narrow-shouldered, black-cloaked figure, its face concealed by a black hood, was striding up the hill toward the house. It was surrounded by a strange aura of darkness, as though it had the ability to repel light itself, and it seemed to be the center from which emanated the ground-trembling, pulsating hum. Behind the awe-inspiring shape the horses belonging to the Portfield bunch were lying on their sides, apparently dead. As Gregg watched, Portfield himself and another man stood up from behind rocks and fired at the figure, using their rifles at point-blank range.

The only effect of their shots was to produce small purple flashes at the outer surface of its surrounding umbra. After perhaps a dozen shots had been absorbed harmlessly, the specter made a sweeping gesture with its left arm, and Portfield and his companion collapsed like puppets. The distance was too great for Gregg to be positive, but he received the ghastly impression that flesh had fallen away from their faces like tatters of cloth. Gregg's own horse whinnied in alarm and bolted away to his right.

Another Portfield man, Max Tibbett, driven by a desperate courage, emerged from cover on the other side of the trail and fired at the figure's back. There were more purple flashes on the edge of the aura of dimness. Without looking around, the being made the same careless gesture with its left arm—spreading the black cloak like a bat's wing—and Tibbett fell, withering and crumbling. If any of his companions were still alive they remained in concealment.

Its cloak flapping around it, the figure drew near the top of the rise, striding with inhuman speed on feet that seemed to be misshapen and disproportionately small. Without looking to left or right, it went straight for the door of Gregg's house, and he knew that this was the hunter from whom Morna had been fleeing. The pervasive hum reached a mind-numbing intensity.

Gregg's previous fear of dying was as nothing compared to the dark dread that spurted and foamed through his soul. He was filled with an ancient and animalistic terror that swept away all reason, all courage, commanding him to cover his eyes and cringe in hiding until the shadow of evil had passed. He looked down at the black, oil-gleaming gun in his hands and shook his head as a voice he had no wish to hear reminded him of a bargain sealed with gold, of a promise made by the man he had believed himself to be. *There's nothing I can do,* he thought. *I can't help you, Morna.*

In the same instant he was horrified to find that he was stepping out from the concealment of the shack. His hands steadied and aimed the gun without conscious guidance from his brain. He squeezed the trigger. There was a brilliant purple flash, which pierced the being's aura like a sword of lightning, and it staggered sideways with a raucous shriek, which chilled Gregg's blood. It turned toward him, left arm rising like the wing of a nightmarish bird.

Gregg saw the movement through the triangular arch of his own forearms, which had been driven back and upward by the gun's recoil. The weapon itself was pointing vertically, and uselessly, into the sky. An eternity passed as he fought to bring it down again to bear on an adversary who was gifted with demonic strength and speed. Gregg worked the trigger again, there was another flash, and the figure was hurled to the ground, shrilling and screaming. Gregg advanced on legs that tried to buckle with every step, blasting his enemy again and again with the gun's enormous power.

Incredibly, the dark being survived the massive blows. It rose to its feet, the space around it curiously distorted, like the image seen in a flawed lens, and began to back away. To Gregg's swimming senses, the figure seemed to cover an impossible distance with each step, as though it were treading an invisible surface that itself was retreating at great speed. The undulating hum of power faded to a whisper and was gone. He was alone in a bright, clean, slow-tilting world.

Gregg sank to his knees, grateful for the sunlight's warmth. He looked down at his chest and was astonished by the quantity of

blood that had soaked through his clothing; then he was falling
forward and unable to do anything about it.

*It is forbidden for me to tell you anything . . . my poor, brave
Billy . . . but you have been through so much on my behalf. The
words will probably hold no meaning for you, anyway—assuming
you can even hear them.*

*I tricked you, and you allowed yourself to be tricked, into tak-
ing part in a war . . . a war that has been fought for twenty thousand years and that may last forever. . . .*

There were long periods during which Gregg lay and stared at
the knotted, grainy wood of the ceiling and tried to decide if it really was a ceiling, or if he was in some way suspended high above
a floor. All he knew for certain was that he was being tended by a
young woman, who came and went with soundless steps, and who
spoke to him in a voice whose cadences were as measured and
restful as the ocean tides.

*We are evenly matched—my people and the Others—but our
strengths are as different as our basic natures. They have superior
mastery of space; our true domain is time. . . .*

*There are standing waves in time . . . all presents are not equal
. . . the "now" that you experience is known as the Prime Present, and has greater potential than any other. You are bound to
it, just as the Others are bound to it . . . but the mental disci-
plines of my people enabled us to break free and migrate to another crest in the distant past . . . to safety. . . .*

Occasionally, Gregg was aware of the dressings on his chest
being changed, and of his lips and brow being moistened with cool
water. A beautiful young face hovered above his own, the gray
eyes watchful and concerned, and he tried to remember the name
he associated with it. Martha? Mary?

*To a woman of my race, the time of greatest danger is the last
week of pregnancy . . . especially if the child is male and destined
to have a certain cast of mind. . . . In those circumstances the
child can be drawn to your "now," the home time of all humanity,
and the mother is drawn with it. . . . Usually she can assert control soon after the child is born and return with it to the time of
refuge . . . but there have been rare examples in which the male*

child resisted all attempts to influence its mental processes, and lived out its life in the Prime Present. . . .

Happily for me, my son is almost ready to travel . . . for the prince has grown clever and would soon return. . . .

His enjoyment of the taste of the soup was Gregg's first indication that his body was making up its losses of blood, that his strength was returning, that he was not going to die. As the nourishing liquid was spooned into his mouth, he filled his eyes with the fresh young beauty of his daughter-wife, and was thankful for her kindness and grace. He forced into the deepest caverns of his mind all thoughts of the dreadful dark hunter who had menaced her.

I'm sorry . . . my poor, brave Billy . . . my son and I must travel now. The longer we remain, the more strongly he will be linked to the Prime Present . . . and my people will be anxious until they learn that we are safe. . . .

I have been schooled to survive in your "now," though in less hazardous parts of it . . . which is why I am able to speak to you in English . . . but my ship came down in the wrong part of the world, all these thousands of years ago, and they will fear I have been lost. . . .

A moment of lucidity. Gregg turned his head and looked through the open door of the bedroom into the house's main living space. Morna was standing at the table, her head surrounded by a vibrant golden halo of hair. She stooped to rest her forehead against that of her child.

They both became hazy, then transparent; then they were gone.

Gregg pushed himself upright in the bed, shaking his head, reaching for them with his free hand. The pain of the reopening wound burned across his chest and he fell back onto the pillows, gasping for breath as the darkness closed in on him again. An indeterminate time later he felt the coolness of a moist cloth being pressed against his forehead, and his crushing sense of loss abated.

He smiled and said, "I was afraid you had left."

"How could I leave you like this?" Ruth Jefferson replied. "What in God's name has been going on out here, Billy Gregg? I find you lying in bed with a bullethole in you, and the place outside looking like a battleground. Sam and some of his friends are out there cleaning up the mess the buzzards left, and they say they haven't seen anything like it since the war."

Gregg opened his eyes and chose to give the sort of answer she would expect of him. "You missed a good fight, Ruth."

"Good fight!" Ruth clucked with exasperation. "You're more of an old fool than I took you for, Billy Gregg. What happened? Did the Portfield mob fall out with each other?"

"Something like that."

"Lucky for you," Ruth scolded. "And where were Morna and the baby when all this was going on? Where are they now?"

Gregg sorted through his memories, trying to separate dream and reality. "I don't know, Ruth. They . . . left."

"How?"

"They went with friends."

Ruth looked at him suspiciously, then gave a deep sigh. "I still think you've been up to something, but I've got a feeling I'll never find out what it was."

Gregg remained in bed for a further three days, being nursed to fitness by Ruth, and it seemed to him a perfectly natural outcome that they should revive their plans to be married. During that time there was a fairly steady stream of callers, men who were pleased that he was alive and that Josh Portfield was dead. All of them were curious about the details of the gun battle, which was fast becoming legendary, but he said nothing to dispel the notion that Portfield and his men had annihilated themselves in a sudden quarrel.

As soon as he had the house to himself, he searched it from one end to the other and found, tucked in behind his whisky jar, six slim gold bars neatly wrapped in a scrap of cloth. In keeping with his expectations, however, the big revolver—the black engine of death—was missing. He knew that Morna had decided he should not have it, and for a while he thought he might understand her reasons. There were words, half remembered from his delirium, that seemed as though they might explain all that had happened. It was only necessary to recall them properly, to get them into sharp focus in his mind. And at first the task appeared simple—the main requirement being a breathing space, time in which to think.

Gregg got his breathing space, but it was a long time before he could accept that, like the heat of summer, dreams can only fade.

Unreasonable Facsimile

Coburn gazed at his girlfriend with a growing sense of dread. He had heard about things like this happening to perfectly normal young women, but he had always considered Erica to be immune.

"You never mentioned marriage before," he said numbly. "Besides—you're a zoologist."

"Implying I have fleas? Or brucellosis?" Erica drew herself up to her full height, bringing her green eyes half an inch above Coburn's. The movement had the effect of making her athletic Swedish body more desirable than ever, but Coburn was reminded of a cobra spreading its hood in menace.

"No, no." He spoke hastily. "All I meant was that somebody in your line of business must be aware of how unnatural the monogamous state is among. . ."

"Animals. Is that how you think of me?"

"Well, you certainly aren't a vegetable or a mineral." Coburn smirked desperately. "I meant that as a joke, sweetie."

"I know you did, darling." Erica softened unexpectedly and leaned toward him, swamping Coburn's senses with impressions of warmth, spun-gold hair, perfume, and mind-erasing curvatures. "But you would enjoy being married to a healthy animal like me, wouldn't you?"

"Of course I . . ." Coburn stopped speaking as he realized what was happening. "The trouble is I *can't* marry you."

"Why not?"

"Well, you see . . ." His mind raced, seeking inspiration. "As a matter of fact . . . ah . . . I've joined the Space Mercantile."

Erica recoiled instantly. "To get away from me!"

"No." Coburn unfocused his eyes, hoping it would give him the appearance of being space-struck. "It's the outward urge, sweetie.

I can't fight it. The wild black yonder's calling to me. My feet are itching to tread the surface of alien stars."

"Planets," Erica said severely.

"That's what I meant to say."

"In that case, I too will go away." Her eyes were magnified by tears. "To forget you."

Coburn was basically a softhearted young man, and he was distressed to see that Erica was upset, but he consoled himself with the thought of having escaped marriage which, as any citizen of the twenty-first century knew, was a tedious anachronism.

He was all the more surprised, therefore, to discover—three days after Erica had left on a field trip to some unpronounceable corner of the world—that life no longer seemed worth living. None of the pleasures that had seemed so attractive when Erica was talking marriage were pleasures any longer.

In the end—deciding he had reached the low point of his life—he did what seemed the only logical thing to do.

He joined the Space Mercantile.

Coburn discovered later that he had been mistaken about the lowest point in his life. This realization came, suddenly, after he had been in the service about three months.

With no previous experience of piloting a spaceship, and no particular aptitude for the work, he had nevertheless been able to get through the basic course in two weeks—thanks to the Universal Cockpit, which was a virtually identical feature in all forms of transport, from cars through airplanes and submarines to space-craft. It allowed a man to concentrate on where he was going instead of on how to get there.

Coburn had been doing just that—concentrating on transferring a cargo of luminous furs between two star systems far out on the Rim—when something cold and metallic was pushed against the back of his neck. His yelp of surprise was occasioned mostly by the discovery that there was a stowaway on his one-man space-ship, but it acquired overtones of alarm as he tentatively decided that the only object a stowaway would thrust against his neck was a gun.

"This is a gun," a hoarse voice confirmed. "Just do what you're told and you won't get hurt."

"All I want to do is get back home, if that's all right with you."

"It isn't." The intruder moved from behind the control chair into Coburn's field of view. He was a thick-set, gingery man, about forty, with a shaven head and even frosting of reddish stubble over his skull and face.

Coburn nodded. "If you'd wanted to get to my base you'd have stayed hidden till the end of the trip?"

"Correct."

"Which means you want me to land somewhere else, I suppose."

"Right again, sonny. Now head for the second world of Toner there." The ginger man tapped a flaring bright spot near one side of the ship's forward viewscreen.

"You don't want to go there—it's uninhabited!"

"That's *why* I want to go there, sonny. I'm Patsy Eckert."

The name brought a momentary loosening of Coburn's bowels. Eckert could not be described as a master criminal—he had been caught too many times for that—but he was wanted on a hundred worlds because he was apparently incapable of performing a lawful action. Larceny, blackmail, rape, and murder were his way of life just as easily and naturally as other men worked and played.

"I thought," Coburn whispered, "that you had been . . ."

"Executed? Not this time. I got away, but I guess I need to hide out for a few years. Somewhere they'd never think of looking for me."

Coburn was not stupid, and he tried to prevent his thought processes from reaching a certain inevitable conclusion concerning his own fate. "But you must be able to find a better hideout." He gestured at the encircling viewscreens. "Look how much space there is in the galaxy. Every one of those thousands of points of light is a planet. . . ."

"A star," Eckert put in, eying Coburn curiously.

"That's what I meant to say. Surely somewhere in those vast empty spaces . . ."

Eckert raised his gun. "Sonny, unless you want some spaces let into your head, put this ship down right where I told you."

Coburn nodded glumly, and began tapping out the instructions that would cause the ship's computer to change course toward the nearest sun and autoland on its second planet. It was obvious that once Eckert had gone to ground he could not permit the ship to proceed on its way, so the best Coburn could hope for was to be kept prisoner on an unexplored planet. The alternative was a quick death shortly after landing. He preserved a moody silence while the ship did a series of dimension slips, the target system blurring and expanding by jumps in the viewscreen until the second world was a saucer-sized disk directly ahead. It was a bland, white orb, completely covered with clouds.

"No landing aids here, so we can't ooze in," Coburn said. "It'll have to be a normal-continuum linear approach."

"Don't worry—I've had this planet in mind a long time. Under that cloud it's just one big grassy plain."

While Coburn was confirming that description on the long-range radar, Eckert moved in behind him again and nudged the muzzle of his gun into the hollow at the base of his skull. Coburn thought wistfully and hopelessly about the state of married bliss in which he could have been living with Erica had he not been so crazy as to leave her and the warm security of Earth. *This is it,* he told himself as the vessel plunged into a roiling, misty atmosphere. *This is the real low point of my life—things just can't get any worse.*

He was wrong again.

As the ship's long, slanting descent brought it through the lower side of the cloud cover, he saw dead ahead—where there should have been only a featureless plain—the massive and strangely familiar shape of a snow-capped mountain.

He barely had time to scream before his ship went straight into a wall of rock.

Coburn regained consciousness to find himself lying on the tilted but undamaged floor of his control room. Eckert was draped across the instrument console, looking both puzzled and shaken. Various electronic monitors were making urgent noises, but the fact that there was enough of them left intact to produce any sound at all was, in Coburn's opinion, an undiluted miracle. He shook his head weakly and was pondering the impossibility of the situation when Eckert retrieved his gun and leveled it once more.

"How did you do it?" the ginger man snarled.

"Do what?"

"Manipulate the dimension slips so that we landed on Earth."

"What gives you a crazy idea like that?"

"Don't fool around, sonny. That mountain we almost hit was Mount Everest."

Coburn was sick, shocked, and angry—and he discovered he no longer cared about the other man's gun. "Try to get it into your head that if I had invented a slip technique capable of doing that I'd be a billionaire and not . . ." His voice dried up as a weird thought struck him. The monstrous edifice of rock he had glimpsed in the foreward screen *had* looked like Mount Everest. He struggled to his feet and looked at the screen, but it and all its companions had been blanked out by the crash. Other thoughts stirred in his mind.

"And I'll tell you something else, mister," he said. "We didn't *almost* hit that mountain—we went straight into the side of it! We should have been vaporized."

Eckert took a deep breath and scowled dangerously. "I happen to know there aren't any mountains on Toner II, so . . ."

An alarm bell clamored, signaling that lethal radioactive materials were escaping from ruptured casings into the ship's living space.

"Sort it out later," Coburn said. "We've gotta get out of here."

He wrenched open an escape door, revealing a vista of steep white slopes, and leaped from the sill down into a snowdrift. Eckert followed a second later, almost landing on top of him. They sat up, breathing cool, resinous air, and looked all around them. The ship lay at the end of a long, shallow gouge, surrounded by the moraines of snow it had built up in its course, and beyond it the stark ramparts of rock soared into a leaden sky. Again Coburn was reminded of Everest—which was almost as peculiar as the fact of still being alive.

"This stuff's warm," Eckert shouted, lifting a handful of white flakes. "It isn't like ordinary snow."

Coburn held some close to his face and saw that the fluffy fragments were more like chips of plastic foam. The thickly resinous smell that seemed to pervade the atmosphere of Toner II cloyed his nostrils, making his head swim.

"Let's get away from the ship," he said uncertainly. "Something might blow."

They trudged away from the slightly crumpled hull, instinctively heading down the slope. A strong breeze was trailing streamers of snow and mist across their vision, but occasionally they caught glimpses of what appeared to be a gray-green plain far below.

"I guess this can't be Earth, after all," Eckert conceded. "Something strange going on, though."

An hour later they had made little progress toward the base of the mountain because the white material on which they were walking, although unlike Earth snow in some respects, was just as slippery underfoot and had a tendency to compress into glassy clumps around their boots. Coburn had lapsed into a dejected silence, broken only by occasional gasps or grunts whenever he lost his balance and fell. He was thinking yearningly about Erica, who was hundreds of light-years away back on Earth, and wondering if she would ever get to hear about his mysterious disappearance, when his ears picked up a distant shout. The wind carried the faint wisp of sound away, but it was obvious from Eckert's face that he had heard it too.

"Over that way," Eckert said, pointing to his left. "There's somebody else here."

They changed course, taking a lateral line across the slope, and in a few minutes Coburn became aware of an area of lime-green brightness illuminating the mists ahead. The light was obviously coming from an artificial source. Coburn's first impulse was to run toward it, but Eckert had his pistol out again and held him back.

"Not so fast, sonny," he said. "I'm not sticking my head into any noose."

They came to a low hillock beyond which the brightness was now very intense. At Eckert's instigation they went down on all fours, crawled to the top, and cautiously peered down the other slope. Barely a hundred paces away, two black posts stood vertically in the snow, about four feet apart. At the base of each was a cluster of cables and metal boxes, and the rectangular area between the posts appeared as a sheet of flickering, crackling radiance, which obscured the section of hillside right behind it. The snow in the vicinity was flattened by numerous footprints. For some reason, Coburn found himself thinking of a portal, a doorway that had been left open.

In a few seconds this impression was reinforced by the abrupt materialization of two brownish, shaggy-furred gorillas, who stepped out of the glowing rectangle and shuffled around, brushing ice droplets from their bodies. Violent flurries of snow spilled out of the rectangle behind them, although—Coburn noticed—the air of Toner II was relatively still, and it was not snowing. He began to get a chilly premonition of the portal's true nature.

"What ugly brutes!" Eckert's voice was a whisper. "Any idea what they are?"

"They aren't on the Mercantile's identification chart, but you know the Earth Federation's only a small part of the Galactic Commune. It contains thousands of cultures we know nothing about."

"The less we know about yugs like those the better," Eckert replied, displaying a chauvinism that—in view of his antagonism to all human standards—Coburn found mildly surprising. "There's more of them. Say, could that thing be a matter transmitter?"

Another four gorillas had appeared, two of them carrying tripod devices that looked vaguely like surveyors' theodolites. One of them began to talk in a loud braying voice, which was so strangely modulated that it took Coburn a few seconds to realize that the creature was speaking Galingua.

". . . from the Chief of Structural Maintenance," the gorilla was saying. "He reported that a small Earth-type vessel made an unscheduled planetfall less than two hours ago. The absorption fields prevented the structure from showing on its radar screens, so it hit the northern face right in the center of the Great Couloir, carried away part of the new heating and refrigeration system, and emerged just above the Khumbu Glacier on the south side."

Another gorilla hopped excitedly. "It went right through! That means it could be lying near here."

"That's why all the survey teams have been called in from Earth to help with the search. All construction work is suspended until we make sure the ship's crew are dead."

"Have we to kill them?"

"If necessary. Then we've to find the ship and shoot it clear of the Toner system before its beacons attract a recovery vessel."

The hopping gorilla slowed down. "Seems a lot of trouble for one primitive ship."

"Not too much. Can you imagine what the Committee would do to us if news about Everest Two got out? Two centuries of work would have gone down the drain!"

Eckert gripped Coburn's shoulder. "Did you hear what he said? He talked about bringing survey teams back from *Earth*—and those brutes have been coming through that green light with survey equipment! I'd say that's a matter transmitter and that I only have to step through it to arrive on Earth."

"I thought you wanted to hide somewhere out of the way," Coburn said numbly, his mind on other things. Disturbing things.

"If I got to Earth instantaneously and without leaving a trail, that would be the best hideout of the lot. Who's going to look there for me?"

Coburn pushed the other man's hand away impatiently. "Who cares? Listen, I've just discovered why we were able to hit a mountain head on and not be killed, and why the air here smells of resin, and why this snow isn't like real snow."

"What's on your mind, sonny?" There was a trace of careless indulgence in Eckert's voice, and his eyes were fixed hungrily on the glowing green rectangle.

"Don't you get it? *These creatures are building a glassfiber replica of Mount Everest!*"

"Balls," Eckert commented in an amiable voice, without turning his head. He lay perfectly still, watching as the group of aliens moved off purposefully. They took a course that led them only slightly to the left of the sheltering hillock, but none of them noticed the two men. As soon as they had vanished into the flurried snow Eckert turned to Coburn, pistol at the ready.

"This is the parting of the ways for us," he said. "I'm going through the green light."

"I want to go, too."

"I darcsay, but you're the one guy who could blow the whistle on me. Sorry." He aimed the pistol.

"Our hairy friends will hear if you shoot me. They could be all around us. They could go after you."

Eckert considered. "That's right. I'd be better to wreck the black boxes on those posts after I'm through and close the door behind me. That'll hold you in the meantime." He thrust the muzzle of the gun into Coburn's solar plexus with the force of a karate blow. Coburn felt the breath driven from his lungs, and—although he remained conscious—his paralyzed thorax refused to take in any more air. He began to worry about dying. Glutinous clicking noises were emerging from his throat as Eckert stood up and, with red-furred head bent low, ran toward the portal.

He had almost reached it when another gorilla stepped through.

Eckert shot the gorilla in the stomach. It sat down with a bump, clutched its middle, then gently fell backward. Honking shouts came from the direction in which the original group had vanished. Eckert glanced all around him, jumped into the green rectangle, and disappeared from view.

Coburn had a sudden conviction that Toner II had become an even more unhealthy place for him to be. So intense was the feeling that he overcame his paralysis and rose to his knees in an effort to reach the portal, but already he could hear the aliens returning, and he knew he could not escape in time. He threw himself down again as running humanoid figures emerged blurrily from the haze. Four of them were of the now-familiar gorilla type, but two were hairless, much thinner, with green-tinted skins partially covered by yellow tunics. Their bald heads glistened like carefully polished apples.

They all gathered around the supine, motionless form of the shot gorilla, talked quietly for a moment, and began to scan the immediate vicinity with fierce, brooding scowls. Coburn abruptly became aware of Eckert's footprints leading directly from the portal to his protective hillock, and a moment later the aliens noticed the same thing. They spread out in a crescent and began to advance on Coburn's position. He was trying to sink into the unyielding ground when there was an unexpected diversion.

Patsy Eckert stumbled back out through the rectangular brilliance of the portal.

He was coated with real snow from head to foot, shivering so violently he could barely stand, and the little to be seen of his face beneath its icy covering had assumed a corpselike pallor. One of the gorillas saw Eckert immediately, gave a shout, and the others ran at him in a bunch. Eckert tried to raise his pistol, but it dropped from his fingers. A hairless creature brought him down with a passable football tackle, and he was lost to view in a confusion of alien bodies and limbs.

In his place of comparative safety, Coburn's ideas about the glassfiber copy of Mount Everest were crystallizing. If his thesis was correct, the portal did not lead to just any random location on Earth—it had to emerge at the corresponding point on the real Everest so that the survey teams could easily transfer their measurements. Eckert therefore had emerged on Mount Everest in the middle of winter, in an environment where a man could live for only a matter of seconds without a heated suit and facemask. Apparently the gorilla beings could survive in those conditions with their long, shaggy coats, and if they had been surreptitiously visiting Earth for a couple of centuries . . .

My God, Coburn thought, *I'm looking at Abominable Snowmen!*

All the old unconfirmed sightings, all the inexplicable footprints in the Himalayan snow, all the legends of the Yeti had originated with these alien creatures who—for reasons of their own—were making a plastic imitation of Earth's highest mountain.

The mystery of the gorillas' motives was threatening to swamp Coburn's mind when he was distracted by new developments near the portal. Ignoring the body of their dead companion, the aliens gathered up the helpless Eckert and carried him away into the green-tinted mists. They passed close by the hillock, again without noticing Coburn. His breathing had returned to normal, and the path was now clear for him to leap through the portal, but he had learned there was no escape that way. He took a sustainer pellet from his belt pouch, sucked on it thoughtfully, and then set off to follow the group of aliens at a discreet distance.

Less than a kilometer along the slope, at an area of rocky

outcroppings, they were met by a party of four of the hairless beings, who stopped to examine the still-shivering form of Patsy Eckert. One of them put his face too close to Eckert, who demonstrated his returning powers of mobility by punching it in the region of the nose. Coburn felt a grudging respect for some aspects of the ginger man's character as he edged near enough to hear what the aliens were saying. He had begun to believe that both types of creature were rather shortsighted, and he felt little sense of immediate danger in wriggling in so close.

". . . by what we found in the ship there were two Earthmen," one of the newly arrived green humanoids was honking in Galingua. "We must find the other before the chief gets here."

"I suppose we'll get the blame as usual," the smallest gorilla complained. "I always said we should have orbital defenses."

"And attract attention? You know how strict the Galactic Games Committee is about infringements of the rules. If they found our mountaineering team practicing the ascent of Everest in advance of the Games we'd be disqualified for a minimum of ten centuries."

The small gorilla was not satisfied. "Why did they have to pick Everest, anyway?"

"You're beginning to sound disloyal, Vello," the hairless alien said. "Everest is an excellent mountain, well up to competition standard. And you know how difficult it is for the Committee's scouts to find a suitable new mountain every five centuries when they can choose only from worlds they are sure will be eligible to join the Galactic Commune before the next Games. It's far from easy, especially when the natives have good eyes and start making UFO searches."

"I still don't think this practice model is worth all the effort."

"My dear boy, you're obviously too young to appreciate the value of the prestige, the enormous political capital a competing world acquires by fielding a winning team." The others joined in, ganging up on the small gorilla. Coburn became so interested in trying to decipher the babble of voices that he incautiously raised his head above the level of the glassfiber rock. A chilling sensation gripped him as he found his eyes met by those of Eckert, who was lying at the aliens' feet. Coburn did not know why he should feel

alarmed at having been seen by the other human, because the gorillas and hairless creatures were now in a full-scale bull session
and had not noticed him. He raised one hand and wiggled the
fingers slightly in a comradely greeting—Eckert had been prepared
to kill him earlier, but now they were two Earthmen on an alien
world, facing a hostile environment together.

"There's the other one," Eckert shouted, pointing straight at
Coburn's rock. "He's hiding over there!"

An abrupt silence descended on the aliens, and they stared my-
opically in Coburn's direction as he sank downward, cursing Eckert
and saying anguished mental good-byes to Erica. Eckert used the
distraction to bolt for freedom. With animal swiftness he scrambled to his feet and darted away. Two aliens grabbed for him, but
he avoided them by easily surmounting a boulder and leaping
down onto the flat ground on the other side. There was a sharp
splintering sound as he went right through the surface. Coburn
glimpsed a jagged black hole from which drifted a despairing
scream, fading and Dopplering away into a low moan. It sounded
as though Eckert was falling a long way down.

"I *knew* there were thin patches around here," one of the gorillas commented. "Mildo's been skimping on materials again."

"Never mind that," a hairless alien said waspishly. "We'd better
check out those rocks." The group fanned out, exactly as they had
done once before, and began converging on Coburn. He lurched to
his feet and ran, instinctively heading back toward the greenish
glow of the portal.

"Get him! Kill him!" an alien shouted. Coburn swore nastily as
he recognized the nasal honk of the smallest gorilla, the one he
had already classified as a troublemaker. Coburn had always been
a pretty good runner, but now—boosted by fear of being caught or
of falling through the surface—he skimmed across the snowscape,
unable to feel any pressure between his feet and the ground. As
the aliens fell behind, the green glow brightened ahead and resolved itself into the familiar glowing portal. The dead gorilla was
still lying close to one of the black posts.

During the early part of his flight Coburn had had a dreamy
conviction that he could run clear around the planet at the same
speed, but now—one kilometer farther on—he was rapidly losing

steam, and the aliens were in full cry not far behind. He staggered up to the portal, put one foot through the rectangular sheet of light, and quickly withdrew it. The Himalayan winter had seized on his flesh like a ravenous animal.

Breathing noisily, mouth filling with the salt froth of exhaustion, he slumped to the ground. His choices were sharply limited—to a fairly quick death in the cold snows of the real Everest, or a possible very quick death at the hands of the aliens on the fake Everest. Coburn chose the latter, mainly because it absolved him from the trouble of standing up again. The shouts of his pursuers grew louder.

This is it, Erica, he thought. *And I did love you.*

He looked around with dispirited eyes, striving for a philosophical calm, but derived little comfort from the unlovely form of the dead gorilla. The long hairs of its coat were stirring listlessly in the breeze, revealing a glint of brassy fittings close to the skin. Ornaments? Coburn crawled over to the inert body, pushed the hairs aside, and discovered a zip fastener running from the creature's chin to its groin.

Glancing up, eyes full of surmise, he saw the vanguard of the hunting party scrambling over rocks in the middle distance. The greenish aliens were in the lead. There was perhaps a minute left to him. He unzipped the gorilla, pushed back its animal facemask, and found one of the bald-headed greenish aliens dead inside. The hairy outer covering had been both a disguise and a protective suit for the illicit excursions to Earth.

Coburn was jabbering with excitement and panic while he hauled the alien out of its cocoon. The cries of his pursuers became more urgent as they saw what he was doing. They were almost on him now. He struggled into the floppy skin, drew the gorilla helmet down over his head, and, without waiting to zipper the suit, jumped through the portal just as a clawing greenish hand raked down his back.

The Himalayan wind, accompanied by an incredible stab of cold, entered through the open front of the gorilla suit. Coburn closed it up, hampered by the clumsiness of his gloved hands, and moved away from the portal, which from this side manifested itself merely as two black posts. The wind was fierce, and he found it almost impossible to keep his balance on the uneven surface, but it was imperative that he put distance between himself and the portal. Those aliens who had been wearing their suits were slower in catching up on him than their unhampered companions had been, but they would come spilling out after him very soon.

Coburn stumbled away into the blinding snowclouds. Within ten minutes he began to feel reasonably safe from capture; an hour later he was absolutely certain he would never see the green-skinned aliens again. The only trouble was that he had begun to suspect he would never see *anybody* again. This was Everest, the awesome king of the Himalayas, howling in elemental triumph all around, and Coburn had neither the experience nor the equipment to get clear.

He kept going, doggedly, heading downward as best he could and hoping the heater elements in his suit were of heavy-duty standard. Gradually, though, his strength began to fail. He began taking more falls and requiring longer to get up. Eventually it was not worth the effort to go on. Coburn sat down on a low rock and waited for the snow to cover him, to blot out all trace of his futile existence. He reconciled himself to facing his eternal rest.

About thirty seconds of eternal rest had passed when a coarsely woven net enveloped his body and pulled him to the ground.

Coburn gave a startled gasp and tried to break free, but the tough cords bound themselves tighter around his arms and legs. The aliens had found him after all, he realized, and this time they were taking no chances. Improvising swear words in Galingua, he fought to stand upright, to die like a man, but even this modest ambition was thwarted when something hit him a crushing blow at the base of the skull. As the light faded from his eyes he noticed that his captors were wearing ordinary human-style snowsuits.

There followed a confused period in which he was partly unconscious but at times aware of being dragged through the snow in the net. When he recovered sufficiently to voice a protest he discovered that the mouth of his gorilla mask had jammed shut, making intelligent speech impossible. Coburn gave up, lay back, and concentrated on avoiding the jagged rocks, which seemed to bestrew the path. A few minutes later the group stopped walking, and one of them opened his faceplate.

"We got one," he called in English to someone outside Coburn's field of view. "We captured a Yeti!"

"How marvelous!" replied a woman.

Coburn's indignation at being classified and treated as an animal faded abruptly as the voice reached his ears. He sat up and began struggling feverishly with his zipper.

The woman knelt in front of him. "A Yeti," she breathed. "My own Yeti!"

Coburn got the zipper undone and pushed back his gorilla helmet. "Erica," he said. "My own Erica!"

"Christ Jesus," she said strickenly. Then her face broke into a radiant smile that even the cold could not dim. "Oh, you foolish, wonderful man! And I really believed you had run away to space and forgotten about me."

"Never," he replied, reaching for her.

"No time for that now." She helped pull him to his feet. "We've got to get you indoors before you freeze. And no doubt you'll have some fantastic story to explain how you came to be following my expedition in an animal suit."

Coburn put his arm around her waist. "I'll try to think of one."

A Full Member of the Club

It was a trivial thing—a cigarette lighter—that finally wrecked Philip Connor's peace of mind.

Angela and he had been sitting at the edge of her pool for more than an hour. She had said very little during that time, but every word, every impatient gesture of her slim hands, had conveyed the message that it was all over between them.

Connor was sitting upright on a canvas chair, manifestly ill at ease, trying to understand what had brought about the change in their relationship. He studied Angela carefully, but her face was rendered inscrutable, inhuman, by the huge insect eyes of her sunglasses. His gaze strayed to a lone white butterfly as it made a hazardous flight across the pool and passed, twinkling like a star, into the shade of the birches.

He touched his forehead and found it buttery with sweat. "This heat is murderous."

"It suits me," Angela said, another reminder that they were no longer as one. She moved slightly on the lounger, altering the brown curvatures of her seminakedness.

Connor stared nostalgically at the miniature landscape of flesh, the territory from which he was being evicted, and reviewed the situation. The death of an uncle had made Angela rich, *very* rich, but he was unable to accept that as sufficient reason for her change in attitude. His own business interests brought him in more than two hundred thousand dollars a year, so she knew he wasn't a fortune hunter.

"I have an appointment in a little while," Angela said.

Connor decided to try making her feel guilty. "You want me to leave?"

He was rewarded by a look of concern, but it was quickly gone, leaving the beautiful face as calm and immobile as before. Angela sat up, took a cigarette from a pack on the low table, opened her purse, and brought out the gold cigarette lighter. It slipped from her fingers, whirred across the tiles, and went into the shallow end of the pool. With a little cry of concern she reached down into the water and retrieved the lighter, wetting her face and tawny hair in the process. She clicked the dripping lighter once, and it lit. Angela gave Connor a strangely wary glance, dropped the lighter back into her purse, and stood up.

"I'm sorry, Phil," she said. "I have to go now."

It was an abrupt dismissal, but Connor, emotionally bruised though he was, scarcely noticed. He was a gypsy entrepreneur, a wheeler-dealer, one of the very best—and his professional instincts were aroused. The lighter had ignited the first time while soaking wet, which meant it was the best he had ever seen, and yet its superb styling was unfamiliar to him. This fact bothered Connor. It was his business to know all there was to know about the world's supply of sleek, shiny, expensive goodies, and obviously he had let something important slip through his net.

"All right, Angie." He got to his feet. "That's a nice lighter—mind if I have a look?"

She clutched her purse as though he had moved to snatch it. "Why don't you leave me alone? Go away, Phil." She turned and strode off toward the house.

"I'll stop by for a while tomorrow."

"Do that," she called, without looking back. "I won't be here."

Connor walked back to his Lincoln, lowered himself gingerly onto the baking upholstery, and drove into Long Branch. It was late in the afternoon, but he went back to his office and began telephoning various trade contacts, making sure they too were unaware of something new and radical in cigarette lighters. Both his secretary and his assistant were on vacation, so he did all the work himself. The activity helped to ease the throbbing hurt of having lost Angela, and—in a way he was unable to explain—gave him a comforting sense that he was doing something toward getting her back or, at least, finding out what had gone wrong between them. He had an illogical conviction that the little gold artifact was somehow connected with their breaking up. The idea was utterly ridiculous, of course; but in thinking back over the interlude by the pool with Angela, it struck him that, amazingly for her, she had gone for a long time without smoking, until that last moment. Although it probably meant she was cutting down, another possibility was that she had not wanted to produce the lighter in his presence.

Realizing that his inquiries were getting him nowhere, he closed up the office and drove across town to his apartment. The evening was well advanced yet seemingly hotter than ever—the sun had descended to a vantage point from which it could attack more efficiently, slanting its rays through the car windows. He let himself into his apartment, showered, changed his clothes, and prowled unhappily through the spacious rooms, wishing Angela was with him. A lack of appetite robbed him of even the solace of food. At midnight he brewed coffee with his most expensive Kenyan blend, deriving a spare satisfaction from the aroma, but took only a few disappointed sips. *If only,* he thought for the thousandth time, *they could make it taste the way it smells.*

He went to bed, consciously lonely, and yearned for Angela until he fell asleep.

The next morning Connor awoke feeling hungry and, while eating a substantial breakfast, he was relieved to find that he had regained his usual buoyant outlook on life. It was perfectly natural for Angela to be affected by the sudden change in her circumstances, but when the novelty of being rich, instead of merely well off, had faded, he would win her back. And in the meanwhile he— the man who had been first in the country with Japanese liquid display watches—was not going to give up on a simple thing like a new type of cigarette lighter.

Deciding against going to his office, he got on the phone and set up further chains of business inquiries, spreading his net as far as Europe and the Far East. By midmorning the urge to see Angela again had become very strong. He ordered his car to be brought around to the main entrance of the building, and he drove south on the coast road to Asbury Park. It looked like another day of unrelieved sunshine, but a fresh breeze from the Atlantic was fluttering in the car windows and further elevating his spirits.

When he got to Angela's house there was an unfamiliar car in the U-shaped driveway. A middle-aged man wearing a tan suit and steel-rimmed glasses was on the steps, ostentatiously locking the front door. Connor parked close to the steps and got out.

The stranger turned to face him, jingling a set of keys. "Can I help you?"

"I don't think so," Connor said, resenting the unexpected presence. "I called to see Miss Lomond."

"Was it a business matter? I'm Millett of Millett and Fiesler."

"No—I'm a friend." Connor moved impatiently toward the doorbell.

"Then you should know that Miss Lomond doesn't live here anymore. The house is going up for sale."

Connor froze, remembering that Angela had said she wouldn't be around, and shocked that she had not told him about selling. "She did tell me, but I hadn't realized she was leaving so soon," he improvised. "When's her furniture being collected?"

"It isn't. The property is going on the market as it stands."

"She's taking *nothing?*"

"Not a stick. I guess Miss Lomond can afford new furniture without too much difficulty," Millett said drily, walking toward his car. "Good morning."

"Wait a minute." Connor ran down the steps. "Where can I get in touch with Angela?"

Millett ran a speculative eye over Connor's car and clothing before he answered. "Miss Lomond has bought Avalon—but I don't know if she has moved in yet."

"Avalon? You mean . . . ?" Lost for words, Connor pointed south in the direction of Point Pleasant.

"That's right." Millett nodded and drove away. Connor got into his own car, lit his pipe, and tried to enjoy a smoke while he absorbed the impact of what he had heard. Angela and he had never discussed finance—she simply had no interest in the subject—and it was only through oblique references that he had been able to guesstimate the size of her inheritance as in the region of a million, perhaps two. But Avalon was a rich man's folly in the old Randolph Hearst tradition, the nearest thing to a royal palace that existed outside Europe, and surrounded by a dozen square miles of the choicest land in Philadelphia. Real estate was not one of Connor's specialties, but he knew that anybody buying Avalon would have had to open the bidding at ten million or more. In other words, Angela was not merely rich, she had graduated into the millionaires' superleague, and it was hardly surprising that her emotional life had been affected.

Connor was puzzled, nevertheless, over the fact that she was selling all her furniture. There was, among several cherished pieces, a Gaudreau writing desk, about which she had always shown an exaggerated possessiveness. Suddenly aware that he could neither taste nor smell the imported tobacco that had seemed so good in his pouch, Connor extinguished his pipe and drove out onto the highway.

He had traveled south for some five miles before admitting to himself that he was going to Avalon.

The house itself was invisible, screened from the road by a high red-brick wall. Age had mellowed the brickwork, but the coping stones on top had a fresh appearance and were surmounted by a climbproof wire fence. Connor drove along beside the wall until it curved inward to a set of massive gates, which were closed. At the sound of his horn, a thick-set man in a uniform of *café-au-lait* gabardine, and with a gun on his hip, emerged from a lodge. He looked out through the gate without speaking.

Connor lowered a car window and put his head out. "Is Miss Lomond at home?"

"What's your name?" the guard said.

"I'm Philip Connor."

"Your name isn't on my list."

"Look, I only asked if Miss Lomond was at home."

"I don't give out any information."

"But I'm a personal friend. You're obliged to tell me whether she's at home or not."

"Is that a fact?" The guard turned and sauntered back into the lodge, ignoring Connor's shouts and repeated blasts on the horn. Angered by the incident, Connor decided not to slink away. He began sounding the car horn in a steady bludgeoning rhythm—five seconds on, five seconds off—but the guard did not reappear. Five minutes later a police cruiser pulled alongside with two state troopers in it, and Connor was moved on, with an injunction to calm down.

For lack of anything better to do, he went to his office.

A week went by, during which time Connor drew a complete blank on the cigarette lighter, and was almost forced to the conclusion that it had been custom-built by a modern Fabergé. He spent hours trying to get a telephone number for Angela, without success. Sleep began to elude him, and he felt himself nearing the boundary that separates rationality from obsession. Finally, he saw a society column picture of Angela in a New York nightspot with Bobby Janke, playboy son of an oil billionaire. Apart from making Connor feel ill with jealousy, the newspaper item provided him with the information that Angela was taking up residence at her newly acquired home sometime on the following weekend.

Who cares? he demanded of his shaving mirror. *Who cares?*

He began drinking vodka tonics at lunchtime on Saturday, veered onto white rum during the afternoon, and by nightfall he was suffused with a kind of alcoholic dharma that told him he was entitled to see Angela and to employ any means necessary to achieve that end. There was the problem of the high brick wall but, with a flash of enlightenment, Connor realized that walls are mainly psychological barriers. To a person who understood their nature as well as he did, walls became doorways. Taking a mouthful of neat rum to strengthen his sense of purpose, Connor sent for his car.

Avalon's main entrance, scene of his earlier defeat, was in darkness when he reached it, but lights were showing in the gate lodge. Connor drove on by, following the line of the wall, and parked on a deserted stretch of second-class road. He switched off all lights, opened the trunk, took out a heavy hammer and chisel, crossed the verge, and—without any preliminaries—attacked the wall. Ten minutes later, although the mortar was soft with age, he had not succeeded in removing one brick and was beginning to experience doubts. Then the first brick came free, and others virtually tumbled out after it. He enlarged the hole to an appropriate size and crawled through onto dry turf.

A dwarfish half moon was perched near the zenith, casting a

wan radiance on the turrets and gables of a mansion that sat on the crest of a gentle rise. The building was dark and forbidding, and as he looked at it Connor felt the warm glow in his stomach fade away. He hesitated, swore at himself, and set off up the slope, leaving his hammer and chisel behind. By bearing to the left he brought the front elevation of the building into view and was encouraged to see one illuminated window on the first floor. He reached a paved approach road, followed it to the Gothic-style front entrance, and rang for admission. A full minute later the door was opened by an archetypal and startled-looking butler, and Connor sensed immediately that Angela was not at home.

He cleared his throat. "Miss Lomond . . ."

"Miss Lomond is not expected until mid . . ."

"Midnight," Connor put in, expertly taking his cue. "I know that—I was with her this afternoon in New York. We arranged that I would stop by for a late drink."

"I'm sorry, sir, but Miss Lomond didn't tell me to expect any visitors."

Connor looked surprised. "Didn't she? Well, the main thing is she remembered to let them know at the gate lodge." He squeezed the butler's arm democratically. "You know, you couldn't get through that gate in a Sherman tank if your name wasn't on the list."

The butler looked relieved. "One can't be too careful these days, sir."

"Quite right. I'm Mr. Connor, by the way—here's my card. Now show me where I can wait for Miss Lomond. And, if it isn't imposing too much, I'd like a daiquiri. Just one to toy with while I'm waiting."

"Of course, Mr. Connor."

Exhilarated by his success, Connor was installed in an enormous green-and-silver room and supplied with a frosty glass. He sat in a very comfortable armchair, sipped his daiquiri, and judged it to be the best he had ever tasted. The sense of relaxation prompted him to reach for his pipe, but he discovered it must have been left at home. He prowled around the room, found a box of cigars on a sideboard, and took one from it. He then glanced around for a lighter. His gaze fell on a transparent ruby-colored ovoid sitting upright on an occasional table. In no way did it resemble any table lighter he had ever seen, but he had become morbidly sensitive on the subject, and the ovoid was positioned where he would have expected a lighter to be. Connor picked it up, held it to the light, and found it was perfectly clear, with no works visible inside. That meant it could not be a lighter. As he was setting it down, he allowed his thumb to slide into a seductively shaped depression on the side.

A pea-sized ball of radiance—like a bead fashioned from sunlight—appeared at the top of the egg. It shone with absolute steadiness until he removed his thumb from the dimple.

Fascinated by his find, he made the tiny globe of brilliance appear and disappear over and over again, and proved its hotness with a fingertip. He took out the pocket magnifier he always carried for evaluating trinkets and examined the tip of the egg. The glass revealed a minute silver plug set flush with the surface, but nothing more. Following a hunch, Connor carefully guided one drop of liquid from his drink onto the egg and made sure it was covering the nearly invisible plug. When he operated the lighter it worked perfectly, the golden bead burning without wavering until the liquid had boiled off into the air.

He set the lighter down and noticed yet another strange property: The ruby egg was smoothly rounded at the bottom, yet it sat upright, with no tendency to topple over. His magnifier showed an ornate letter P engraved in the base, but provided no clue as to how the balancing act was achieved.

Connor gulped the remainder of his drink and, with eyes that suddenly were sober and watchful, took a fresh look around the room. He discovered a beautiful clock, apparently carved from solid onyx. As he had half expected, there was no way to open it, and the same elaborate P was engraved on the underside.

There was also a television set that had a superficial resemblance to an expensive commercial model but that bore no maker's name plaque. He checked it over and found the now-familiar P inscribed on one side, where it would never be noticed except by a person making a purposeful search. When he switched the set on, the image of a newscaster that appeared on the screen was so sharp and perfect that he might have been looking through a plate-glass window into the man's face. Connor studied the picture from a distance of only a few inches and could not resolve it into lines or dots. His magnifier achieved no better results.

He switched the television off and returned to the armchair, filled with a powerful and strange emotion. Although it was in his nature to be sharp and acquisitive—those were attributes without which he could never have entered his chosen profession—it had always remained uppermost in his mind that the world's supply of money was unlimited, whereas his own allocation of years was hopelessly inadequate. He could have trebled his income by working longer and pushing harder, but he had always chosen another course simply because his desire for possessions had never taken control. However, that had been before he discovered the sort of possessions that real money could buy. He knew he was particularly susceptible to gadgets and toys, but the knowledge did nothing to lessen the harsh, raw hunger he now felt. And there was no way that anybody was going to stop him from joining the ranks of those who could afford future-technology artifacts. He would prefer to do it by marrying Angela, because he loved her and would enjoy sharing the experiences, but if she refused to have him back, he would do it by making the necessary millions himself.

A phrase that had been part of his train of thought isolated itself in his mind: *future technology*. He weighed the implications for a moment, then shrugged them off—he had lost enough mental equilibrium without entertaining fantasies about time travel.

The idea was an intriguing one, though, and it answered certain questions. The lighters he coveted, partly for their perfection and partly because they could earn him a fortune, were technically far in advance of anything on the world's markets, yet it was within the realms of possibility that a furtive genius was producing them in a back room somewhere. But it was hard to see how the impossibly good television set could have been manufactured without the R&D facilities of a powerful electronics concern. The notion that they were being made in the future and shipped back in time was only slightly less ridiculous than the idea of a secret industry catering exclusively for the superrich.

Connor picked up the cigar and lit it, childishly pleased at having a reason to put the ruby egg to work. His first draw on the cool smoke gave him the feeling that he had been searching for something all his life and suddenly had found it. Cautiously at first and then with intense pleasure, he filled his lungs with the unexpected fragrance. He luxuriated. This was smoking as it was idealized in tobacco company commercials—not the shallow, disappointing experience commonly known to smokers everywhere. He had often wondered why the leaf that smelled so beguiling before it was lit, or when someone nearby was smoking, promising sensual delights and heart's ease, never yielded anything more than virtually tasteless smoke.

They promise you "a long, cool smoke to soothe a troubled world," Connor thought, *and this is it.* He took the cigar from his mouth and examined the band. It was of unembellished gold and bore a single ornate *P.*

"I might have known," he announced to the empty room. He looked around through a filigree of smoke, wondering if everything in the room was different from the norm, superior, better than the best. Perhaps the ultrarich scorned to use *anything* that was available to the man-in-the-street or advertised on television or . . .

"Philip!" Angela stood in the doorway, pale of face, shocked, and angry. "What are you doing here?"

"Enjoying the best cigar I've ever had." Connor got to his feet, smiling. "I presume you keep them for the benefit of guests—I mean, a cigar is hardly your style."

"Where's Gilbert?" she snapped. "You're leaving right now."

"Not a chance."

"That's what you think." Angela turned with an angry flail of blond hair and cerise skirts.

Connor realized he had to find inspiration and get in fast. "It's too late, Angela. I've smoked your cigar, I lit it with your lighter, I have checked the time with your clock, and I've watched your television."

He had been hoping for a noticeable reaction and was not disappointed—Angela burst into tears. "You fool! You had no *right!*"

She ran to the table, picked up the lighter, and tried to make it work. Nothing happened. She went to the clock, which had stopped going; and to the television set, which remained lifeless when she switched it on. Connor followed her circuit of the room, feeling guilty and baffled. Angela dropped into a chair and sat with her face in her hands, huddled and trembling like a sick bird. The sight of her distress produced a painful churning in his chest. He knelt in front of Angela.

"Listen, Angie," he said. "Don't cry like that. I only wanted to see you again—I haven't done anything."

"You touched my stuff and made it change. They told me it would change if anybody but a client used it—and it has."

"This doesn't make sense. Who said what would change?"

"The suppliers." She looked at him with tear-brimmed eyes, and all at once he became aware of a perfume so exquisite that he wanted to fall toward its source like a suffocating man striving toward air.

"What did you . . . ? I don't . . ."

"They said it would all be spoiled."

Connor tried to fight off the effects of the witch magic he had breathed. "Nothing has been spoiled, Angie. There's been a power failure . . . or something . . ." His words tailed away uncertainly as he remembered that the clock and the television set were cordless. He took a nervous drag on the half-smoked cigar and almost gagged on the flat, acrid taste of it. The sharp sense of loss he experienced while stubbing it out seemed to obliterate all traces of his skepticism.

He returned to Angela's chair and knelt again. "They said this stuff would stop working if anybody but you touched it?"

"Yes."

"But how could that be arranged?"

She dabbed her eyes with a handkerchief. "How would I know? When Mr. Smith came over from Trenton he said something about all his goods having an . . . essence field, and he said I had a molecular thumbprint. Does that make sense?"

"It almost does," Connor whispered. "A perfect security system. Even if you lost your lighter at the theater, when somebody else picked it up it would cease to be what it was."

"Or when somebody breaks into your home."

"Believe me, it was only because I had to see you again, Angie. You know that I love you."

"Do you, Philip?"

"Yes, darling." He was thrilled to hear the special softness return to her voice. "Look, you have to let me pay for a new lighter and television and . . ."

Angela was shaking her head. "You couldn't do it, Philip."

"Why not?" He took her hand and was further encouraged when she allowed it to remain in his.

She gave him a tremulous smile. "You just couldn't. The installments are too high."

"Installments? For God's sake, Angie, *you* don't buy stuff on time."

"You can't buy these things—you pay for a service. I pay installments of $864,000."

"A year?"

"Once every forty-three days. I shouldn't be telling you all this, but . . ."

Connor gave an incredulous laugh. "That comes to about six million a year—nobody would pay that much."

"Some people would. If you even have to think about the cost, Mr. Smith doesn't do business with you."

"But . . ." Connor incautiously leaned within range of Angela's perfume, and it took his mind. "You realize," he said in a weak voice, "that all your new toys come from the future? There's something fantastically wrong about the whole setup."

"I've missed you, Philip."

"That perfume you're wearing—did it come from Mr. Smith, too?"

"I tried not to miss you, but I did." Angela pressed her face against his, and he felt the coolness of tears on her cheek. He kissed her hungrily as she moved down from the chair to kneel against him. Connor spun toward the center of a whirlpool of ecstasy.

"Life's going to be so good when we're married," he heard himself saying after a time. "Better than we could ever have dreamed. There's so much for us to share and . . ."

Angela's body stiffened and she thrust herself away from him. "You'd better go now, Philip."

"What is it? What did I say?"

"You gave yourself away, that's all."

Connor thought back. "Was it what I said about sharing? I didn't mean your money—I was talking about life . . . the years . . . the experiences."

"I could never be sure of that."

"I loved you before you even knew you would inherit a cent."

"You never mentioned marriage before."

"I thought that was understood," he said desperately. "I thought you . . ." He stopped speaking as he saw the look in Angela's eyes. Cool, suspicious, disdainful. The look that the very rich had always given to outsiders who tried to get into their club without the vital qualification of wealth.

She touched a buzzer and continued standing with her back to him until he was shown out of the room.

The ensuing days were bad ones for Connor. He drank a lot, realized that alcohol was no answer, but went on drinking. For a while he tried getting in touch with Angela, and even drove down to Avalon. The brickwork had been repaired at the point where he had made his entry, and a close inspection revealed that the entire wall was newly covered with a fine mesh. He had no doubt that tampering with it in any way would trigger off an alarm system.

When he awoke during the night he was kept awake by hammering questions. What was it all about? Why did Angela have to make such odd payments, and at such odd intervals? What would men from the future want with twentieth-century currency? On several occasions the thought occurred that, instead of concentrating on Angela, he would do better to find the mysterious Mr. Smith of Trenton. The flicker of optimism the idea produced was quenched almost immediately by the realization that he simply did not have enough information to provide a lead. It was a certainty that the man was not even known as Smith to anybody but his clients. If only, while shocked into talking, Angela had revealed something more—like Smith's business address.

Connor returned each time to brooding and drinking, careless of the fact that his behavior was becoming completely obsessive. Then he awoke one morning to the discovery that he already knew Smith's business address, had known it for a long time, almost from childhood.

Undecided as to whether his intake of white rum had hastened or delayed the revelation, he breakfasted on strong coffee and was too busy with his thoughts to fret about the black liquid being more tasteless than ever. He formulated a plan of action during the next hour, twice lighting his pipe—out of sheer habit—before remembering that he was finished with ordinary tobacco forever. As a first step in the plan he went out, bought a five-inch cube of ruby-colored plastic, and paid the owner of a jobbing shop an exorbitant sum to have the block machined down to a polished ovoid. It was late in the afternoon before the work was finished, but the end product sufficiently resembled a *P*-brand table lighter to fool anyone who was not looking too closely at it.

Pleased with his progress thus far, Connor went back to his apartment and dug out the .38 pistol he had bought a few years earlier following an attempted burglary. Common sense told him it was rather late to leave for Trenton and that he would be better off waiting until morning, but he was in a warmly reckless mood. With the plastic egg bumping on one hip and the gun on the other, he drove westward out of town.

Connor reached the center of Trenton just as the stores were showing signs of closing for the day. His sudden fear of being too late, and of having to wait another day after all, was strengthened by the discovery that he was no longer so certain about locating Mr. Smith.

In the freshness of the morning, with an alcoholic incense lingering in his head, it had all seemed simple and straightforward. For much of his life he had been peripherally aware that in almost every big city there are stores that have no right to be in existence. They were always small and descreet, positioned some way off the main shopping thoroughfares, and their signs usually bore legends—like "Johnston Bros." or "H&L"—which seemed designed to convey a minimum of information. If they had a window display at all it tended to be nothing more than an undistinguished and slightly out-of-style sports jacket priced three times above what it had any chance of getting. Connor knew that the stores were not viable propositions in the ordinary way because, not surprisingly, nobody ever went into them. And yet in his mind they were, in some indefinable way, associated with money.

Setting out for Trenton, he had been quite sure of the city block he wanted—now at least three locations and images of three unremarkable storefronts were merging and blurring in his memory. *That's how they avoid attention,* he thought, refusing to be disheartened, and began cruising the general area he had selected. The rush of homegoing traffic hampered every movement, and finally he decided he would do better on foot. He parked in a side street and began hurrying from corner to corner, each time convincing himself that he was about to look along a remembered block and see the place he so desperately wanted to find, but each time being disappointed. Virtually all the stores were closed by now, the crowds had thinned away, and the reddish evening sunlight made the quiet, dusty façades look unreal. Connor ran out of steam, physically and mentally.

He swore dejectedly, shrugged, and started limping back to his car, choosing—as a token act of defiance—a route that took him a block farther south than he had originally intended going. His feet were hot and so painful that he was unable to think of anything but his own discomfort. Consequently he did a genuine double-take when he reached an intersection, glanced sideways, and saw a half-familiar, half-forgotten vista of commonplace stores, wholesalers' depots, and anonymous doorways. Connor's heart began a slow pounding as he picked out, midway on the block, a plain storefront whose complete lack of character would have rendered it invisible to eyes other than his own.

He walked toward it, suddenly nervous, until he could read the sign, which said GENERAL AGENCIES, in tarnished gold lettering. The window contained three pieces of glazed earthenware sewer pipe, beyond which were screens to prevent anyone from seeing the store's interior. Connor expected to find the door locked, but it opened at his touch, and he was inside without even having had time to prepare himself. He blinked at a tall, gaunt man who was standing motionless behind a counter. The man had a down-curving mouth, ice-smooth gray hair, and something about him gave Connor the impression that he had been standing there, unmoving, for hours. He was dressed in funeral director black, with a silver tie, and the collar of his white shirt was as perfect as the petals of a newly opened flower.

The man leaned forward slightly and said, "Was there something, sir?"

Connor was taken aback by the quaintness of the greeting, but he strode to the counter, brought the ruby egg from his pocket, and banged it down.

"Tell Mr. Smith I'm not satisfied with this thing," he said in an angry voice. "And tell him I demand a repayment."

The tall man's composure seemed to shatter. He picked up the egg, half turned toward an inner door, then paused and examined the egg more closely.

"Just a minute," he said. "This isn't . . ."

"Isn't what?"

The man looked accusingly at Connor. "I've no idea what this object is, and we haven't got a Mr. Smith."

"Know what *this* object is?" Connor produced his revolver, confident he had seen and heard enough to justify taking a harder line.

"You wouldn't dare to shoot me."

"No?" Connor aimed the revolver at the other man's face and, aware that the safety catch was on, gave the trigger an obvious squeeze. The tall man shrank against the wall. Connor muttered furiously, clicked the safety off, and raised the gun again.

"Don't!" The man shook his head. "I beseech you."

Connor had never been beseeched in his life, but he did not allow the curious turn of speech to distract him. He said, "I want to see Mr. Smith."

"I'll take you to him. If you will follow me. . . ."

They went through to the rear of the premises and down a flight of stairs that had inconveniently high risers and narrow treads. Noting that his guide was descending with ease, Connor glanced down and saw that the tall man had abnormally small feet. There was another peculiarity about his gait, but it was not until they had reached the basement floor and were moving along a corridor that Connor realized what it was: Within the chalk-stripe trousers, the tall man's knees appeared to be a good two thirds of the way down his legs. Cool fingers of unease touched Connor's brow.

"Here we are, sir." The black-clad figure before him pushed open a door. Beyond it was a large, brightly lit room, and at one side was another tall, cadaverous man dressed like a funeral director. He too had ice-smooth gray hair, and he was carefully putting an antique oil painting into the dark rectangular opening of a wall safe.

Without turning his head, he said, "What is it, Toynbee?"

Connor slammed the door shut behind himself. "I want to talk to you, Smith."

Smith gave a violent start, but continued gently sliding the gold-framed painting into the wall. When it had disappeared he turned to face Connor. He had a down-curved mouth and—even more disturbingly—his knees, also, seemed to be in the wrong place. *If these people come from the future,* Connor thought, *why are they made differently from us?* His mind shied away from the new thought and plunged into irrelevant speculations about the kind of chairs Smith and Toynbee must use—if any. He realized that he had seen no seats or stools about the place. With a growing coldness in his veins, Connor recalled his earlier impression that Toynbee had been standing behind the counter for hours, without moving.

". . . welcome to what money we have," Smith was saying, "but there's nothing else here worth taking."

"I don't think he's a thief," Toynbee went and stood beside him.

"Not a thief! Then what does he want? What is . . . ?"

"Just for starters," Connor put in, "I want an explanation."

"Of what?"

"Of your entire operation here."

Smith looked mildly exasperated. He gestured at the wooden crates that filled much of the room. "It's a perfectly normal agency setup handling various industrial products on a . . ."

"I mean the operation whereby you supply rich people with cigarette lighters that nobody on this Earth could manufacture."

"Cigarette lighters? I'm afraid . . ."

"The red egg-shaped ones that have no works, but they light when they're wet and stand upright without any support."

Smith shook his head. "I wish I *could* get into something like that."

"And the television sets that are too good. And the clocks and cigars and all the other things that are so perfect that people who can afford it are willing to pay $864,000 every forty-three days for them—even though the goodies are charged with an essence field that fades out and converts them to junk if they fall into the hands of anybody who isn't in the club."

"I don't understand a word of this."

"It's no use, Mr. Smith," Toynbee said. "Somebody has talked."

Smith gave him a venomous stare. *"You* just did, you fool!" In his anger Smith moved closer to Toynbee, so that his body was no longer shielding the wall safe. Connor noticed for the first time that it was exceptionally large, and then it occurred to him that a basement storeroom was an odd place for that particular type of safe. He looked at it more closely. The darkness of the interior revealed no trace of the oil painting he had just seen loaded into it. And, far into the tunnel-like blackness, a bright green star was throwing off expanding rings of light, rings that faded as they grew.

Connor made a new effort to retain his grasp of the situation. He pointed at the safe and said, casually, "I assume that's a two-way transporter."

Smith was visibly shaken. "All right," he said, after a tense silence, "who talked to you?"

"Nobody." Connor felt he could get Angela into trouble of some kind by mentioning her name.

Toynbee cleared his throat. "I'll bet it was that Miss Lomond. I've always said you can't trust the *nouveau riche*—the proper instincts aren't sufficiently ingrained."

Smith nodded in agreement. "You're right. She got a replacement table lighter, television, and clock—the things this . . . person has just mentioned. She said they had been detuned by someone who broke into her house."

"She must have told him everything she knew."

"And broken her contract—make a note of that, Mr. Toynbee."

"Hold on a minute," Connor said loudly, brandishing the revolver to remind them he was in control. "Nobody's going to make a note of anything till I get the answers I want. These products you deal in—do they come from the future or somewhere?"

"From somewhere," Smith told him. "Actually, they come from a short distance in the future as well, but—as far as you are concerned—the important thing is that they are transported over many light-years. The time difference is incidental, and quite difficult to prove."

"They're from another planet?"

"Yes."

"You, too?"

"Of course."

"You bring advanced products to Earth in secret and sell or rent them to rich people?"

"Yes. Only smaller stuff comes here, of course—larger items, like the television sets, come in at main receivers in other cities. The details of the operation may be surprising, but surely the general principles of commerce are well known to you."

"That's exactly what's bothering me," Connor said. "I don't give a damn about other worlds and matter transmitters, but I can't see why you go to all this trouble. Earth currency would be of no value on . . . wherever you come from. You're ahead on technology, so there's nothing . . ." Connor stopped talking as he remembered what Smith had been feeding into the black rectangle: an old oil painting.

Smith nodded, looking more relaxed. "You are right about your currency being useless on another world. We spend it here. Human culture is primitive in many respects, but the race's artistic genius is quite remarkable, even by interstellar standards. Our organization makes a good trading surplus by exporting paintings and sculptures. You see, the goods we import are comparatively worthless."

"They seem valuable to me."

"They *would* seem that way to you—that's the whole point. We don't bother bringing in the things that Earth can produce reasonably well. Your wines and other drinks aren't too bad, so we don't touch them. But your coffee!" Smith's mouth curved even further downward.

"That means you're spending millions. Somebody should have noticed one outfit buying up so much stuff."

"Not really. We do quite a bit of direct buying at auctions and galleries, but often our clients buy on our behalf, and we credit their accounts."

"Oh, no," Connor breathed as the ramifications of what Smith was saying unfolded new vistas in his mind. Was this why millionaires, even the most unlikely types of men, so often became art collectors? Was this the *raison d'être* for that curious phenomenon, the private collection? In a society where the rich derived so much pleasure from showing off their possessions, why did so many art treasures disappear from the public view? Was it because their owners were trading them in against *P*-brand products? If that was the case, the organization concerned must be huge, and it must have been around for a long time. Connor's legs suddenly felt tired.

He said, "Let's sit down and talk about this."

Smith looked slightly uncomfortable. "We don't sit. Why don't you use one of those crates if you aren't feeling well?"

"There's nothing wrong with me, so don't try anything," Connor said sharply, but he sat on the edge of a box while his brain worked to assimilate shocking new concepts. "What does the *P* stand for on your products?"

"Can't you guess?"

"Perfect?"

"That is correct."

The readiness with which Smith was now giving information made Connor a little wary, but he pressed on with other questions that had been gnawing at him. "Miss Lomond told me her installments were $864,000—why that particular figure? Why not a million?"

"That *is* a million—in our money. A rough equivalent, of course."

"I see. And the forty-three days?"

"One revolution of our primary moon. It's a natural accounting period."

Connor almost began to wish that the flow of information would slow down. "I still don't see the need for all this secrecy. Why not come out in the open, reduce your unit prices, and multiply the volume? You could make a hundred times as much."

"We have to work underground for a number of reasons. In all probability the various Earth governments would object to the loss of art treasures, and there are certain difficulties at the other end."

"Such as?"

"There's a law against influencing events on worlds that are at a sensitive stage of their development. This limits our supply of trade goods very sharply."

"In other words, you are crooks on your own world and crooks on this one."

"I don't agree. What harm do we do on Earth?"

"You've already named it: You are depriving the people of this planet of . . ."

"Of their artistic heritage?" Smith gave a thin sneer. "How many people do you know who would give up a Perfect television set to keep a da Vinci cartoon in a public art gallery five or ten thousand miles away?"

"You've got a point there," Connor admitted. "What have you got up your sleeve, Smith?"

"I don't understand."

"Don't play innocent. You wouldn't have talked so freely unless you were certain I wouldn't get out of here with the information. What are you planning to do about me?"

Smith glanced at Toynbee and sighed. "I keep forgetting how parochial the natives of a single-planet culture can be. You have been told that we are from another world, and yet to you we are just slightly unusual Earth people. I don't suppose it has occurred to you that other races could have a stronger instinct toward honesty, that deviousness and lies would come less easily to them than to humans?"

"That's where we are most vulnerable," Toynbee put in. "I see now that I was too inexperienced to be up front."

"All right, then—be honest with me," Connor said. "You are planning to keep me quiet, aren't you?"

"As a matter of fact, we do have a little device . . ."

"You don't need it," Connor said. He thought back carefully

over all he had been told, then stood up and handed his revolver to Smith.

The good life was all that he had expected it to be, and—as he drove south to Avalon—Connor could feel it getting better by the minute.

His business sense had always been sharp, but whereas he had once reckoned a month's profits in thousands, he now thought in terms of six figures. Introductions, opportunities, and deals came thick and fast, and always it was the P-brand artifacts that magically paved the way. During important first contacts he had only to use his gold lighter to ignite a pipeful of P-brand tobacco—the incredible leaf that fulfilled all the promise of its "nose," or glance at his P-brand watch, or write with the pen that produced any color at the touch of a spectrum ring, and all doors were opened wide. The various beautiful trinkets were individually styled, but he quickly learned to recognize them when they were displayed by others, and to make the appropriate responses.

Within a few weeks, although he was scarcely aware of it, his outlook on life had undergone a profound change. At first he was merely uneasy or suspicious when approached by people who failed to show the talismans. Then he became hostile, preferring to associate only with those who could prove they were safe.

Satisfying though his new life was, Connor had decided it would not be perfect until Angela and he were reunited. It was through her that he had achieved awareness, and only through her would he achieve completeness. He would have made the journey to Avalon much sooner but for the fact that there had been certain initial difficulties with Smith and Toynbee. Handing over the revolver had been a dangerous gambit, which had almost resulted in his being bundled through their matter transmitter to an unknown fate on another world. Luckily, however, it had also convinced them that he had something important to say.

He had talked quickly and well that evening in the basement of the undistinguished little store. Smith, who was the senior of the pair, had been hard to convince; but his interest had quickened as Connor enumerated all the weaknesses in the organization's procurement methods. And it had grown feverish when he heard how

Connor's worldly know-how would eliminate much of the wasteful financial competition of auctions, would streamline the system of purchasing through rich clients, and would institute foolproof controls and effective new techniques for diverting art treasures into the organization's hands. It had been the best improvisation of his life, sketchy in places because of his unfamiliarity with the art world, but filled with an inspired professionalism that carried his audience along with it.

Early results had been so good that Smith had become possessive, voicing objections to Connor's profitable side dealings. Connor smoothed things over by going on to a seven-day work schedule in which he also worked most evenings. This had made it difficult to find the time to visit Angela, but finally his need to see her had become so great that he had pushed everything else aside and made the time.

The guard at the gate lodge was the same man as before, but he gave no sign of remembering his earlier brush with Connor. He waved the car on through with a minimum of delay, and a few minutes later Connor was walking up the broad front steps of the house. The place looked much less awesome to Connor but, while ringing for admission, he decided that he and Angela would probably keep it, for sentimental reasons as much as anything else. The butler who answered the door was a new man, who looked rather like a retired seaman, and there was a certain lack of smoothness in his manner as he showed Connor to the large room where Angela was waiting. She was standing at the fireplace with her back to the door, just as he had last seen her.

"Angie," he said, "it's good to see you again."

She turned and ran to him. "I've missed you so much, Phil."

As they clung together in the center of the green-and-silver room, Connor experienced a moment of exquisite happiness. He buried his face in her hair and began whispering the things he had been unable to say for what seemed a long, long time. Angela answered him feverishly all the while he spoke, responding to the emotion rather than the words.

It was during the first kiss that he became aware of a disturbing fact. She was wearing expensive yet ordinary perfume—not one of the *P*-brand distillations of magic to which he had become accustomed on the golden creatures he had dated casually in the past few weeks. Still holding Angela close to him, he glanced around the big room, and a leaden coldness began to spread through his body. Everything in the room was, like her perfume, excellent—but not Perfect.

"Angela," he said quietly, "why did you ask me to come here?"

"What kind of a question is that, darling?"

"It's a perfectly normal question." Connor disengaged from her and stepped back suspiciously. "I merely asked what your motives were."

"*Motives!*" Angela stared at him, color fleeing from her cheeks, then her gaze darted to his wristwatch. "My God, Philip, you're *in!* You made it, just like you said you would."

"I don't know what you mean."

"Don't try that with me—remember, I was the one who told it all to you."

"You should have learned not to talk by this time."

"I know I should, but I didn't." Angela advanced on him. "I'm out now. I'm on the outside."

"It isn't all that bad, is it? Where's Bobby Janke and the rest of his crowd?"

"None of them come near me now. And you know why."

"At least you're not broke."

She shook her head. "I've got plenty of money, but what good is it when I can't buy the things I want? I'm shut out, and it's all because I couldn't keep myself from blabbing to you, and because I didn't report the way you were getting on to them. But you didn't mind informing on me, did you?"

Connor opened his mouth to protest his innocence, then realized it would make no difference. "It's been nice seeing you again, Angela," he said. "I'm sorry I can't stay longer, but things are stacking up on me back at the office. You know how it is."

"I know exactly how it is. Go on, Philip—take yourself out of here."

Connor crossed to the door, but hesitated as Angela made a faint sound.

She said, "Stay with me, Phil. Please stay."

He stood with his back to her, experiencing a pain that slowly faded. Then he walked out.

Late that afternoon Connor was sitting in his new office when his secretary put through a call. It was Smith, anxious to discuss the acquisition of a collection of antique silver.

"I called you earlier but your girl told me you were out," he said, with a hint of reproach.

"It's true," Connor assured him. "I was out of town—Angela Lomond asked me down to her place."

"Oh?"

"You didn't tell me she was no longer a client."

"You should have known without being told." Smith was silent for a few seconds. "Is she going to try making trouble?"

"No."

"What did she want?"

Connor leaned back in his chair and gazed out through the window, toward the Atlantic. "Who knows? I didn't stay long enough to find out."

"Very wise," Smith said complacently.

When the call had ended, Connor brewed some *P*-brand coffee, using the supply he kept locked in the drinks cabinet, and the perfection of it soothed from his mind all the last lingering traces of remorse.

How on Earth, he wondered idly, *do they manage to make it taste exactly the way it smells?*

The Silent Partners

At first he could see nothing about her except that she was dressed in furs, then that her hair was blond and, in spite of the night wind, as smooth as glass. When the woman drew nearer he made out the glitter of jewelry at her ears and throat, and of gold at her wrists. Then he could see her face, which was beautiful. He did not know the woman, and yet her face was almost familiar, like that of someone he might have dreamed of a long time ago.

Purvey crouched in the utter darkness of the bushes and waited for her to come within reach.

From where he had stationed himself he could see both lamplit entrances to the tiny park, and something of the quiet suburban streets beyond. It was strange then that he had not noticed the woman come through the gates, but perhaps he had overdone it with the whisky while he was waiting. It was years now since he had had to go out and actually rob somebody, and his nerves had needed damping down with alcohol. The outlook in the confidence business was pretty bleak when a practitioner of twenty years' standing had to resort to outright robbery.

Taking a deep breath, he slid the pistol from his pocket and quickly stepped out onto the path. "Don't make a sound," he warned the woman. "Just hand over your purse and that stuff you're wearing." He stared into her face, trying to gauge whether she was the type to do as she was told or the unpredictable, troublesome variety of customer.

In the dim light coming from the street, Purvey saw that something had gone terribly wrong with the beautiful face. His hand flew nervously to his mouth and he took a step backward, raising the pistol protectively.

The woman sagged bonelessly, crumpled, withered away in a

second, leaving nothing but a small dark object writhing on the
ground at Purvey's feet. With a moan of sheer despair he turned to
run.

He was much too late.

Purvey very rarely dreamed, but when he was twelve years old
he had once had a nightmare in which he had committed suicide
by lying in a coffin with earth and roses in it. The thorns had
pierced his flesh and drawn the blood from him—making the roses
flourish and bloom—until he had been sucked dry and was lying
dead beneath a beautiful living shroud of blossoms. Then, as one
can do in dreams, he had realized he did not want to commit suicide, after all.

He had that same feeling now.

Huge fleshy leaves and dozens of dark green tendrils lay across
his chest and face, stirring slightly in the wind and sending explor-
atory trickles of cold water into his clothing. Summoning all his
strength, he pushed the tangled mass aside, sat up, and realized at
once that he was aboard a spaceship. He had been to the Lan-
grangian colonies in moon orbit enough times to enable him
to recognize the sensation, even though his surroundings looked
less like the interior of a spaceship than almost anything else he
had seen.

The low, almost circular room was brilliantly lit from the ceiling
in some places and dark in others, giving an impression of shad-
owy vastness quite out of keeping with its true size. The walls were
dark brown and streaming with moisture. Large fans, positioned at
intervals around the walls, were making random-seeming movements on their bearings and creating a cold, irregular wind.

The floor was covered with a thin coating of mud from which
jutted a disorderly clutter of instrument pedestals, machine housings, cables, and low partitions. There appeared to be nobody in
the room but himself.

Purvey scrambled to his feet, almost fell with dizziness, and
made his way over to one of the instrument stands, which was
emitting a red glow and a peculiar high-pitched whistle, which
kept changing in tone. On the pedestal was a small screen depict-
ing a few brilliant stars against a background of crimson space.

The markings on the dials were little blobs of many different colors.

He made a circuit of the room, assuring himself that it was empty; then he began shouting for someone to come to let him out. Nobody came. Purvey was feeling dizzier by the minute, as though the air contained some insidious intoxicant. He crossed the room, falling once on the slippery mud, and stood staring down at the little viewscreen, wondering how he had gotten into the nightmarish predicament.

All at once his memory of recent events iced into sharp focus in his mind—the woman in the park! How could he have forgotten that hideously dissolving face or the way she had turned into the indescribable thing on the ground? He ran his fingers over the smooth glass of the viewscreen, feeling slightly relieved at the realization that she, it, was not in the immediate vicinity.

Something behind him made a wet, slithering sound.

Purvey spun around, feeling his mouth drag itself out of shape with fear. The dark green stuff that had been spilling across his face and chest when he awoke had come crawling after him, leaving a broad trail behind it in the mud. In the center of the mass of leaves and tendrils Purvey glimpsed a complicated, knobbly core about half a meter in diameter. Some of the tendrils ended in shiny black beads, which looked as though they might serve the function of eyes.

Purvey backed away from the thing and felt in his pocket for the pistol. It was not there. When a wall ended his retreat he stood staring at the moving growth as it labored toward him propelled by some dimly seen agitation under its core. It stopped advancing when it was about one human pace away from him and remained motionless for what seemed to Purvey a long, long time. Then he noticed that—across one huge leaf on top of the mass—faint letters bleached out in a lighter green had appeared.

The thing was trying to communicate with him.

"You will have gold," the letters spelled out. The black-beaded tendrils waved gently in the air, and the odor of the thing reached up to Purvey—the smell of dusty ivy growing on a decaying wall.

Purvey, responding to one of his favorite words, was immediately less apprehensive. "What for?" He sank down onto his heels and tried to peer into the depths of the apparently intelligent vegetation. "Why will I have gold?"

Another long pause ensued, then the green writing faded and was replaced by, "Explosion wrecked part of ship," then, "including repair shop," then, "Lurr has made rough repairs," then, "You are highly mobile," then, "You will stand by during trip," then, "Lurr will pay with gold."

"I don't know how to repair spaceships," Purvey pointed out, playing for time in which to think.

"The work will be simple. You are mobile. I will direct you." The sentences took a long time to come across by means of the thing's, Lurr's, controlled etiolation effect.

Purvey groped around in his pocket and found a flattened pack of cigarettes and a permatch. When he struck the match it burned with a large, brilliant flame, and he guessed that the air in the ship was loaded with oxygen. That might explain why he felt so dizzy, almost drunk. He blew out the match with some difficulty, put it away, and drew deeply on the cigarette, relishing it.

"Will you take me back to Earth afterward?"

"Yes."

Purvey considered asking Lurr to promise, but decided against it, as he had no way of knowing how much the vegetable's word was worth. It might be no more trustworthy than some of his friends.

"I'd like to know how you got me here," he said. "It seemed a bit . . . sort of unethical." *Not the sort of behavior one would expect from a salad citizen,* he thought reprovingly, but there was no reply to his question. He noticed that the black beads had dulled, as though Lurr had gone to sleep. Purvey snorted disgustedly. He crouched against the wall, coat collar turned up, and finished his cigarette. The only sound in the room was the restless whispering of the fans on the wall above.

Some time later, after a period of uneasy sleep, Purvey woke up with a new problem.

The vinelike growths that formed the extensions of Lurr's body were draped wetly across him, as they had been on his first awakening. He ended the distasteful intimacy by pushing the dark green mass away, trying to understand why it came near him at all.

He was pretty sure that Lurr was as sexless as a cabbage, and yet its touch had something of the quality of a ghastly, yearning caress. Was it possible for a plant to become perverted? Purvey found something particularly unpleasant in the thought of being violated by a vegetable.

"Listen," he said suspiciously, "how long will the trip last?"

A broad leaf unfurled, and the labored writing appeared. "Fifteen of your days."

"What about food?" Purvey demanded. "I'll need food."

"You shall share the Ahtaur's food."

"Ahtaur? What's that?"

"Ahtaur is a helper. She brought you here."

"I don't want her food," Purvey said, suddenly afraid.

"Ahtaur will not mind." Lurr stirred slowly and moved away, leaving a trail through which could be seen the whitish metal of the floor beneath. There were small perforations in it and, as Purvey watched, more mud welled up through them until the metal was covered.

Purvey followed Lurr, wondering if its last remark had been some kind of a sarcasm. Could a thing like Lurr have a sense of humor? Purvey hoped not. It was bad enough to be touched up in his sleep by a sex-starved broccoli without it going around making wisecracks afterward.

Reaching a little door low down on a bulkhead, Lurr extended a tendril, touched a white circle, and the door opened, revealing a plain, cupboardlike interior. At the touch of another circle, a hatch opened in the rear surface, and a block of pink spongy material slid out. Purvey picked it up warily, but he had been hungry long before his current misfortunes had begun, and he had little trouble bringing himself to taste the strange food. It was slightly warm, chewy, and tasted like lobster paste with a strong dash of red pepper. It was better than he had expected.

When he had finished eating, Purvey obtained a rather unsatisfactory drink from one of the little rivulets of water that ran down the walls at intervals. Lurr had gone to one of his instrument panels and was lying motionless beside it, eyestalks extended and poised over the array of meters.

By constant questioning Purvey learned that the ship he was on was a kind of scout, which had been escorting a huge interstellar liner or battleship. When the accident had occurred, rather than have the mother ship stop to give assistance, Lurr had radioed that it would be possible for the scout to reach base unaided. If the scout failed to return, however, the mother ship would come back to find it. Lurr's race only fought wars when attacked by aggressors, but their battleships were very big and powerful.

Purvey noted that the last statement echoed various utterances made by human politicians in the United Nations, and he began to wonder if it had been intended as some kind of a hint. For the possessor of such an alien mind, to say nothing of the body housing it, Lurr seemed to have an excellent control of the English language and did not waste many words.

"How is it," Purvey asked, "that you speak, I mean write, English so well?"

But the black beads were dull again. He wandered around the room looking at the alien mechanisms, flapping his arms to keep warm, and trying to decide what was wrong about the place. It was *all* wrong, of course, being the product of the thinking of an alien life form. But there was another wrongness.

Purvey found that he got tired easily. Time dragged by in the monotonous discomfort of the room, and he slept often, crouched in the darkest corner, where there was the least mud. This was the place where the explosion had occurred, as was evidenced by the seared metalwork, dented machine housings, and shattered ceiling lights. Purvey liked it best because it was the one place that Lurr seemed to avoid.

Once, when he was feeling particularly miserable and Lurr was in one of its unresponsive moods, he decided to look for something in which to wrap himself for warmth. His showerproof was heavy with mud, wet and useless as a garment, and he found himself longing for heat in any form.

He went to the row of low doors and opened several of them by pressing the white circle, which was a common feature. Inside he found perfectly normal shelves stacked with unmarked boxes or machine parts which, although beaded with moisture, showed no signs of corrosion. One shelf was loaded with hundreds of blocks of colored glass or plastic, another with what looked like purple seaweed.

A larger door had a red circle on it. Numb with the cold, Purvey opened the door and saw a little room, in the center of which glowed an old-fashioned pot-bellied stove. He was stooping to cross the threshold when it occurred to him that the stove just could not be there, and he jarred to a halt. Something moved near his feet. Just before he jumped back and slammed the door, he had a blurry vision of a fat, sluglike creature rearing up with gray mouth agape.

Lurr was suddenly conscious again, holding up his communicative leaf. "I see you recognized the Ahtaur this time."

"This time?" Purvey said, "Was that the woman I saw?"

Lurr seemed quite active and alert as the sentences appeared in answer, noticeably quicker than before. The Ahtaur was a very slow-moving, carnivorous animal indigenous to Lurr's home planet. It got close to its victims by telepathically invading their minds and controlling the visual centers to make itself appear attractive to them. Apparently, Lurr had muzzled the Ahtaur, fitted it with something he described as a force-field grab, and lowered it to Earth to find a human being in a quiet and lonely place. Purvey, who liked quiet and lonely places, had walked into the trap.

As a by-product of their study of the Ahtaur's ability, Lurr's people had been able to develop a device that enabled them to detect and comprehend the thoughts of intelligent animals. Purvey eyed his green companion speculatively, rubbing the stubble on his chin and wondering if he had picked up another note of warning.

On the fifth day, reckoned by his wristwatch, Purvey discovered that Lurr had been telling him lies.

His feeling that there was a subtle wrongness in the setup finally culminated in the realization that there were two entirely separate sets of controls in the room. The set that was in use, and at which Lurr spent most of its time, was grouped along one wall. Every part of it, every short pedestal and housing, was constructed with smooth, brilliant metal and with the high standard of workmanship that Purvey associated with good pinball machines. The joints in the metal were barely discernible, and the little colored dots that

Lurr used instead of numbers were perfect circles and squares etched into the metal.

The unused set of controls was scattered over the center of the floor area and, in contrast, reminded Purvey of a radio he had built during a course of remedial training. There were plates that did not fit, unfilled holes, bolts that bolted nothing, and the colored markings were roughly shaped blobs of enamel. Scooping away some handfuls of mud, he found that holes had been burned in the floor to let associated cables and pipes pass through.

None of these earmarks of a jerried-up experimental rig agreed with Lurr's picture of a standard scout ship serving as an operational vessel. But it was hard to see the alien's point in deceiving him over a thing like that. He carefully refrained from thinking about his discovery in case Lurr *should* be able to read his mind and, acting on principle, he began to take an interest in the operation of the ship. His professional instincts told him he might have stumbled onto something good.

Another day went by, speeded now by routine. At intervals Lurr drew some of the pink spongy stuff from the locker and pushed it through a slot in the door of the Ahtaur's room. The dangerous little creature seemed to have about the same status as a pet dog in Lurr's life, except that it was never allowed out for its equivalent of a walk. Purvey helped himself to the same food any time he was hungry and found he was growing to like it.

"This stuff is okay once you get used to it," he told Lurr, waving his hand, which had become sunburned since the start of the trip. "If you get me the recipe I'll buy a restaurant with my gold when I get back, and make it a speciality of the house."

"One of the factors in your enjoyment of the Ahtaur's food," Lurr replied, "is your ignorance of its constituents."

Purvey broke off chewing and threw the remains of his meal into the highly efficient garbage disposal unit that Lurr had allocated to him for various personal uses. He stared at Lurr with brooding eyes, again wondering if he was being laughed at, and wishing he could lay his hands on a spray can of paraquat.

It occurred to him that the leafy alien was quite different to what it had been at the start of the journey. In their occasional conversations, for instance, Lurr could print up his little messages faster than Purvey could answer them, and it gave him an uncomfortable suspicion that the mobile vegetable was more intelligent than he. Lurr's movements had become increasingly more rapid until he could get around as fast as Purvey—another thing Purvey did not quite like. The only change for the better was that Lurr seemed to have gotten over the strange urge to drape himself over Purvey every time he slept. This made Purvey's rest more comfortable.

On the seventh day it occurred to Purvey that he must be further from Earth than anyone had ever been before. Only two manned ships from Earth had reached Mars, so far, although there had been much talk of sending a third ship to see why the first two had not returned. And here was Don Purvey halfway to a star. . . .

"Just how far have we come now?" he asked. "Pretty far, eh? How many light-years?"

"I am not used to calculating in your units," Lurr replied. "The best approximation I can give you is . . . six light-hours."

"Light-*hours!*" Purvey shouted. "But that means we've just crossed the orbit of Pluto. You told me the trip would take fifteen days. Half that time is gone, and yet we're still in the Solar System. What's the game?"

Lurr did not answer at once, the first hesitancy for days. Finally, "The journey is in three stages. Getting clear of your planetary system takes up half the time, entering my own home system will take up the other half. That is traveling in normal space with standard drive.

"The intersystem jump—using Lurrian drive—takes only a few hours."

Purvey rubbed his beard and grinned down at Lurr. *So that's it,* he thought triumphantly. "The new stuff you added to this ship converted it from an ordinary planet-hopper to a starship. You invented it, didn't you, Lurr? Of course! You just mentioned Lurrian drive. You're all alone—there's no big mother ship to look for you. . . ."

The speed of the alien's rush took him by surprise, and Lurr had almost reached the Ahtaur's door before Purvey realized what was happening. He ran after it, muttering angrily, but one of

Lurr's tendrils flicked out and touched the red circle. As the door swung open, Purvey tried to stop, skidded in the mud, and went down heavily on his side. The impact of the fall drove the breath from his lungs.

Purvey gasped noisily as he saw the Ahtaur writhe into the room with unexpected speed, pale gray mouth opening and contracting hungrily. Enveloping it were faint, changing ghosts of formless objects created as its camouflaging talent reacted on Purvey's whirling brain. He glanced around in panic, saw nothing he could use for a weapon, then scrambled for the row of lockers nearest to him.

He opened the door to a compartment and found it was the one full of little glass blocks. The next one contained what appeared to be a complicated valve assembly, and Purvey snatched it from its brackets. The massive piece of metal almost wrenched itself from his grasp as he swung, but he managed to guide it down onto the Ahtaur's back. The sluglike body burst open, and the valve sank down into it. A bubbling moan came from the Ahtaur, and the flickering images that had been blurring its outlines abruptly vanished.

Leaving his improvised club where it was, Purvey turned in search of Lurr. The alien was slithering rapidly toward him with a spiky, cactuslike growth extended in front of it. Purvey leaped back, realizing he should have been less squeamish about retrieving his club. He ran across the room, fumbling under his coat until he had taken off the belt of his trousers. It was of thin, flexible metal. Gripping the buckle tightly, he turned and lashed out with the belt and, luckily, connected with several of Lurr's upraised eye tendrils.

There was a sharp clicking sound as two of the severed eyes hit a partition. Swinging the belt with frightened, loathing haste, Purvey struck again and again until all the eyes were gone. After that the job was comparatively safe, but it took him half an hour—using a strip of torn metal from the wrecked part of the room—to make sure that Lurr was dead.

I'll never eat cole slaw again, he vowed to himself as he gathered up the mass of still-twitching herbage and loaded it into the disposal unit.

The operation of the ship was, as Purvey had learned by watching Lurr, fully automatic. It was a relatively simple matter for him to cancel the instructions under which the ship's computers were steering it out of the Solar System. On a little stylized model of a planetary system, in which a row of buttons was ranged out in a line from a glowing hemisphere, he pressed the third one out to designate Earth. He was betting that the ship would home in on the third planet of any system in this way. The fact that the computer was accustomed to Lurr's home system made no difference because, even there, if the ship was deactivated for any length of time the planetary arrangement would have altered when it was put into use again, making it necessary for the ship to scan the heavens afresh and select its destination.

It was a first-class spaceship, Purvey congratulated himself, hundreds of years ahead of anything on Earth. For the gadget that made it invisible to radar alone he would be able to get more money than he could ever use—and without having to trust his life to any perambulating plant, either.

When he had satisfied himself that he could control the ship, he crouched contentedly in his favorite corner and had his first really peaceful sleep in days. On wakening he found he had a slight headache, which he wrote off as an aftermath of all he had been through, but it continued to get worse as the hours went by. After a meal and another sleep he had to admit, even to himself, that the air in the room had gone stale.

Looking around for air conditioning, he found a little grill in the wall below each fan, which meant there was machinery to regenerate the air as it was used up, and that it had stopped working. Sweating a little in spite of the cold, he searched around and discovered a large duct leading into the wall. The duct emerged from a machine housing near the corner where Purvey slept. And going over to it he discovered a simple, deadly fact—the sides of the housing had been smashed in by the force of the explosion.

The air-conditioning machine was wrecked.

Sobbing with fear, Purvey ran to get tools—then stopped dead. The realization came to him that even if the machinery had been as good as new he would still be in the same predicament. For when it was working it had produced carbon dioxide!

All at once he had the whole picture. Lurr had been a mobile vegetable existing by photosynthesis—converting carbon dioxide and water into carbohydrates, and giving off oxygen in the process. An explosion had wrecked his carbon dioxide production plant during the experimental flip in the starship, so he had obtained a replacement—Don Purvey. That explained Lurr's eagerness to lie close to him at first, and the excess of oxygen in the atmosphere at the start of the flight. It also explained why Lurr had speeded up so much when Purvey had been around for a while breathing out precious carbon dioxide. It had been keeping Lurr alive, and the oxygen Lurr had given off in return had been keeping Purvey alive.

For the operation of a small spaceship, Lurr and Purvey had been a perfect team—and he now realized that it had been a mistake to dissolve the partnership.

As before, he was much too late.

Element of Chance

The summons was far from welcome.

Only that morning Cytheron had turned the world to glass. Not objectively, although he would one day reach a stage where such things would be possible, but subjectively—by modifying his vision to utilize neutrinos and no other form of radiation. He had attempted the same thing without success some centuries earlier, and the memory of the previous failure was contributing to his present enchantment. It made him aware of the processes of his own maturation.

His body was transparent now, sensed only as an interaction of its elements with the mesons of the cosmic ray bombardment. He saw himself as a wisp of organized light moving across the face of a crystal globe, within which the geological strata appeared to writhe like luminous vapors.

Above him the sky was strange. His eyes could peer into the hearts of giant red suns, yet were aware of no other stars. He was exalted, inhaling reality and breathing out its varied aspects as a liquescence of music and poetry.

A day, a year, a decade—all would have been as one in the new sensory configuration. But it seemed that only seconds had passed when the summons arrived, written on daylight, keyed to the singularities of his own cerebral rhythms so that no other denizen of this world could be aware of it except, perhaps, as an impression that a fleeting cloud had crossed the sun. Cytheron readjusted his vision until he became normally aware of his surroundings. He was on a sloping plain where dry, snowlike flakes of amethyst swirled down from a green sky, not to lie dormant, but to flow and coalesce in the currents of invisible magnetic rivers. Beyond the plain was a mountain range of milk-white rock, split in places by fluorescing glaciers.

He was able to orientate.

Cytheron reached out with his mind and *skorded*. In an instant he was standing on another plain far across the world, close to a group of eight elder thanii, members of his own species. There was no snow here—instead, a warm amethyst rain paraded in regular curtains and broke in translucent archways above the group's individual screens. A herd of indigenous six-legged animals cropped the lacy grass all around, but so that the beasts would not be alarmed or disturbed in any way, the thanii were permitting light to pass through their bodies. Cytheron immediately adopted the same mode.

I answer your summons, he thought. *Why did you call?*

You must know. The eight elders thought as with one mind—a unison that never failed to fill Cytheron with dread. *You have come of age, and the group mind is ready to receive you.*

But . . . Cytheron's protest remained stillborn as he realized the truth of what was being said. He had come of age. A thousand years and more glimmered in his memory like dissolving dreams. *I'm not ready.*

You are ready. The group thought was kind but inflexible. *And we are ready to receive you into the group mind.*

I have no doubt that you are prepared to receive me—but what shall I gain in exchange for my youth?

Your racial heritage of experience and wisdom.

Which means I shall become old, doesn't it, elder thanii?

You cannot conceive what you shall become, Cytheron—and therein lies the source of your apprehension. You must have faith in the ways of our kind. You must believe that we know best—and now prepare to be assimilated.

Never!

Cytheron *skorded* as he formed the thought, and at once he was back on the opposite side of the world, haloed by amethyst flakes of desiccated snow. The distant mountains wavered slightly, a sign that the thanii were reaching out and focusing on a location close to him. Then they were with him again, invading his mind with cool remorse. He cried aloud and *skorded* at random—now there was a brown riverbed darkly rolling, amber spires of an amber city sipping the morning sun, and a blue forest's introspective hush—but the elders overtook him easily, and his fear grew.

A strange peacefulness burgeoned within him. He experienced a subtle *melting* and realized he had almost surrendered his identity to the group, had almost yielded his individuality. His despair took him outward from the face of the planet. He paused briefly on the third moon, but the shattered silver daggers of the horizon began to waver, and he knew he had not escaped. Another leap—a giant world's saffron sands under a crimson sky; leap—white hell, heart of a moribund sun; leap—sentient hill of black jelly shifting restlessly beneath cold stars.

And all the time the elder thanii's hold grew firmer.

Cytheron experienced a single moment of insanity. Before fully understanding what he was doing, he had *skorded* to the one place in that region of the galaxy where nobody—in his opinion, not even the thanii—could reach him.

Having endured the fantastic death throes peculiar to its species, the quasar was at peace.

The process of extinction had begun aeons earlier, when the incredibly massive body exhausted its nuclear energy potential and started collapsing radially. Density increased during the contraction until the attendant gravitic field became so fierce as to imprison all radiation, and the quasar's own light began to orbit around it. But the same contraction brought with it a spasmodic renewal of life: Gravitational energies became available, racking the sphere with explosions, which repeatedly pushed its radius back outside the limit at which radiation is trapped.

For ten times a thousand years the quasar fluctuated between two diameters—one above and one below the critical dimension. Since there is no way of communicating with or receiving information from an object that imprisons its emanations, the quasar could be considered as periodically entering and leaving the normal continuum.

Finally, however, even the fund of gravitic energy was depleted. The quasar folded the stuff of space-time in around itself and vanished forever.

Only a silent black hole of gravity marked its position in the stellar concourse.

Cytheron realized the enormity of his mistake almost at once. The surface of the quasar was an inferno of introverted, recirculated energy—but the thanii had long ago learned the secret implicit in the universal truth that without resistance there can be no force, and he was physically at ease. It was a short and relatively simple step from making his body transparent to light to allowing all forms of radiation to pass through it unhindered. The concern he felt sprang from the discovery that he was trapped.

His ability to *skord* was unimpaired, but its effectiveness was canceled by the awesome distortions the quasar had produced in the geometries of reality. Cytheron could *skord* any imaginable distance—but only in a straight line—and in the vicinity of the dead quasar, a straight line was part of a circle. He could reach any point on the quasar's surface instantaneously, but he could conceive of no way to leave it.

All at once, union with the elder thanii—so repugnant a short time earlier—seemed infinitely desirable. It came to Cytheron that he was little more than a child, and that he had behaved with a child's arrogance and intolerance. The summit of his conceit had come when he had accused the elders of trying to take rather than give. In the anguish of self-knowledge, he came close to allowing the laminar flow of pent energy to scatter his body to the white winds of hell.

Be calm, Cytheron, the elder thanii's corporate thought said. *That is not the way.*

You've found me!

Cytheron was overwhelmed with relief as he turned and saw the group of eight, looking hearteningly familiar and composed.

It was not difficult. You have much to learn.

I know. I know. He abased himself fervently. *And I beg that the first thing you show me is the method of* skording *through this barrier of gravity. I have no desire to remain here any longer.*

That is understandable—but there is no way to skord *through such a barrier.*

What? Then I . . . all of us are trapped.

That is not the case. We will destroy the barrier.

The multiple thought of the elder thanii was calm, and Cytheron began to get his first real inkling of the magnitude of their combined intellect.

But how can it be done?

Part of the matter comprising this sphere must be reconstituted as antimatter—the annihilation energy resulting will be sufficient to scatter its mass over a large volume of space, thus dispersing the gravitic field.

You can do this?

We can. The process has already begun.

But . . . The vastness of the operation appalled Cytheron. *You are creating a supernova. Nearby star systems could be triggered off—worlds with life on them might be engulfed. I would prefer not to be freed on those terms. I would die rather than cause the death of another being.*

The thanii reassured him. *Do not be alarmed, Cytheron. We elders have lost none of our reverence for the counterentropic force. Had freeing you meant the destruction of other life, of even one individual, we would have decided to leave you on this sphere. However, you were lucky. There will be the equivalent of a supernova, but the only star close enough to be triggered off is without planets.*

The neutron flux will be intense throughout the entire region, Cytheron persisted. *Will no inhabited worlds be affected?*

None. As we said, you have been very lucky, Cytheron. We examined all the stars in this neighborhood and have found only one evolving system. It has nine worlds—but all are in a very early stage of development, and life will not begin there until long after the violence of the explosion has abated.

I see. I am glad.

Cytheron sought a way to express his gratitude, but all his powers of thought were temporarily lost as antimatter was created at the hands of the elder thanii, and the outraged universe fell upon it in a blaze of attritive fury.

The elders had been correct in their analysis of his fears, Cytheron realized.

He had not been able to conceive what he would become after the assimilation of his identity into the group mind. Nothing in his previous state of separateness could have prepared him for the translation into the adult state of being, its sense of completeness and belonging, its transcendental peace. The sapience and experience of a thousand centuries surrounded him like a luminous cloud, modifying and yet at the same time establishing and reasserting his uniqueness.

He paused briefly near an unremarkable sun with nine planets—the star system closest to the stellar holocaust the thanii had engineered on his behalf. The sun and its retinue of nascent worlds swam undisturbed in the galactic tide, unaware of the cosmic storm approaching them at a large fraction of the speed of light.

As you see, Cytheron, the group mind thought, *there is no life here. The planetary masses are in an early stage of formation.*

I do see. He indicated a globe with an unusually large moon, third from the sun. *I imagine that this one will best approximate the optimum conditions for intelligent life.*

We agree.

I must eventually return here, Cytheron thought. *I can't help feeling some curiosity about the way in which life will develop on this world. I also feel a certain responsibility.*

Responsibility?

Yes. There is no life here yet, but I dread the thought that the consequences of my behavior may have some adverse effect on its future course. After all, the very structure of the planet will be changed when it encounters the neutron flux from the supernova.

You worry unduly, Cytheron, the group mind informed him with amusement tempered by its thousand centuries of wisdom. *The only physical effect the explosion will have on this world is that there will be a high degree of neutron capture, leading to the formation of rather heavier elements than are normally found on a world of that type.*

As he sensed the elder thanii's amusement and was drawn deeper into the group mind, Cytheron felt his unformed fears lesson and vanish. He could find nothing in that almost limitless fund of knowledge to suggest that the development of an intelligent species could be affected—in any noticeable way—by the presence of heavy metals such as gold. Or uranium.

The Gioconda Caper

It was a Thursday morning in January—stale and dank as last night's cigar butts—and my office phone hadn't rung all week. I was slumped at the desk, waiting out a tequila hangover, when this tall, creamy blonde walked in. The way she was dressed whispered of money, and what was inside the dress hinted at my other hobby —but I was feeling too lousy to take much notice.

She set a flat parcel on my desk and said, "Are you Phil Dexter, the private psi?"

I tipped back my hat and gave her a bleak smile. "What does it say on my office door, baby?"

Her smile was equally cool. "It says Glossop's Surgical Corset Company."

"I'll *kill* that signwriter," I gritted. "He promised to be here this week for sure. Two months I've been in this office, and . . ."

"Mr. Dexter, do you mind if we set your problems on one side and discuss mine?" She began untying the string on the parcel.

"Not at all." Having lost the initiative, I decided it would be better to improve customer relations. I never saw much sense in private psis trying to talk and act like private eyes, anyway. "How can I help you, Miss . . . ?"

"I'm Carole Colvin." Her brow wrinkled slightly. "I thought you psi people knew all that sort of thing without being told."

"It's a wild talent," I said in a hollow voice, giving my stock response. "There are forces beyond the control of mere humans."

It was always necessary at this point to look sort of fey and hag-ridden, so I stared out through the fanlight and thought about the lawsuit my ex-secretary was bringing against me for non-payment of wages. Carole didn't seem to notice. She finished unwrapping her parcel, took out an unframed oil painting, and propped it in front of me.

"What can you tell me about this painting?" she said briskly.

"It's a good copy of the 'Mona Lisa,'" I replied. "A very clever imitation, but . . ." My voice faded away of its own accord as the full blast from the canvas hit my extra senses. There was an impression of great age, perhaps five hundred years, and a blurring rush of images—a handsome bearded man in medieval costume, hilly landscapes with dark green vegetation, bronze sculptures, thronged narrow streets of antique cities. Behind this montage, almost obliterated by its brilliance, was the suggestion of a dark place and of a circular wooden frame that might have been part of a large machine.

Carole was regarding me with interest. "It isn't a copy, is it?"

I dragged my jaw back up to its normal position. "Miss Colvin, I'm just about certain this painting was done by Leonardo da Vinci himself."

"You mean it's *the* 'Mona Lisa'?"

"Well . . . yes." I gazed at the canvas, paralyzed with awe.

"But that isn't possible, is it?"

"We'll soon see." I pressed the button on my computer terminal and said, "Has the 'Mona Lisa' been stolen from the Louvre in Paris?"

The reply came with electronic swiftness. "I cannot answer that question."

"Insufficient data?" I said.

"Insufficient funds," the machine replied. "Until you pay your last three quarterly subscriptions you're getting no more information out of me."

I made a rude sign out through the window in the direction I imagined the central computer to lie. "Who needs you?" I sneered. "It would have been in all the papers if the 'Mona Lisa' had been stolen."

"Then, more fool you for asking," the machine said. I took my finger off the button and smirked desperately at Carole, wishing I hadn't tried to put on a display of computerized efficiency.

She looked at me with what seemed to be increasing coldness.

"If you are quite finished, I'll tell you how I got the painting. Or don't you want to hear?"

"I want to. I want to." Realizing I was in danger of losing her business, I sat up straight, looking poised and alert.

"My father was an art dealer, and he had a small gallery up in Sacramento," Carole said, folding herself into a chair with an action like honey flowing from a spoon. "He died two months ago and left the business to me. I don't know much about art, so I decided to sell the whole thing. It was when the inventory was being made up that I found this painting hidden in a safe."

"Nice stroke of luck."

"That remains to be seen. The painting might be worth a few million, or it might be worth a few years in the pen—I want to find out which."

"And so you came to me! Very wise, Miss Colvin."

"I'm beginning to wonder about that. For somebody who's supposed to have a sixth sense, you seem a bit deficient in the other five."

I think that was the moment I fell in love with Carole. The reasoning was that if I could enjoy looking at her while being treated like an idiot child, life should get pretty interesting if I could get her to regard me as an intelligent man. I started on that private project there and then.

"Your father never mentioned the painting to anybody?"

"No—that's what makes me wonder if something illegal was going on."

"Have you any idea how he got it?"

"Not really. He was on vacation in Italy last spring, and I remember he seemed rather odd when he got back."

"In what way?"

"Tense. Withdrawn. Not what you'd expect after a vacation."

"Interesting. Let's see if I can pick up something more to go on." I leaned forward and touched the slightly crazed surface of the painting. Once more there was a strong psychic impulse—images of a balding man I knew to be Carole's father, bright glimpses of cities. The latter would have been unknown to me had they not been accompanied by the intuitions that elevate the psi talent and make it roughly equal to a course in chiropody as a viable means of earning a crust.

"Rome," I said. "Your father went to Rome first, but he spent most of his time in and around Milan."

"That's correct." Carole gave me a look of grudging approval. "It appears that you do have some genuine ability."

"Thanks. Some people think I have nice legs, too." Her compliment was partly lost on me because I had again half-seen a dark place, like a cavern, and a circular wooden machine. There were distracting undertones of mystery and centuries-old secrets.

"We're not much farther on, though," Carole said.

"I thought we were doing pretty well."

"You haven't answered the big question: Did Leonardo paint the 'Mona Lisa' *twice?*"

"That's the way it seems to me, Miss Colvin. I don't know how this will affect the value of the original."

"The original?"

"I mean, the other one." I stared at the painting in awe, letting its sheer presence wash over my senses; then I began to get a feeling there was something not quite right about it, something difficult to put a finger on. The "Mona Lisa" stared back at me, the famous smile playing about her lips just as I remembered it from all the prints I'd seen. Her face was exactly right, the rich medieval background was exactly right, and yet there was some detail of the picture that seemed out of place. Could it, I wondered, be something to do with those plump, smooth hands? To impress Carole, I assumed a look of deep, brooding concentration and tried to decide what it was in the painting that was ringing subconscious alarm bells.

"Have you fallen asleep?" Carole said, rapping the desk with an imperious knuckle.

"Of course not," I replied huffily, and pointed at the "Mona Lisa's" hands. "Do these look right to you?"

"You think you could have done better?"

"I mean, in the Louvre painting does she not have one hand sort of cradled in the other one? Instead of separated like that?"

"Could be—I told you I don't know anything about art."

"It might explain the existence of two 'Mona Lisas.'" I began to warm to my theory. "Perhaps he did this one and then decided it would have been better with the hands in repose."

"In that case," Carole said reasonably, "why didn't he just paint the hands over again?"

"Ah . . . well . . . yes." I swore at myself for having concocted such a dumb theory. "You've got a point there."

"Let's go." Carole got to her feet and began wrapping the painting in its brown paper covering.

"Where to?"

"Italy, of course." A look of impatience flitted across her beautiful features. "I'm employing you to find out if this painting is legally mine, and it's quite obvious you won't be able to do it sitting here in Los Angeles."

I opened my mouth to protest, then realized that the assertive Miss Colvin was right in what she said, that I needed some of the money she so obviously had, and that a spell in the Mediterranean sun would probably do me a lot of good. There was also a powerful element of curiosity about both the painting itself and that part of my psi vision I hadn't yet mentioned to her—the dark cavern and its enigmatic, wheel-like machine.

"Yes?" Carole challenged. "You were going to say something?"

"Not me. I'll be glad to wave good-bye to this place for a few days. How do you say *arrivederci* in Italian?"

We caught the noon suborbital to Rome, were lucky with a shuttle connection, and by early evening had checked into the Hotel Marco Polo in Milan.

The traveling had made me hungry, and I did justice to the meal that Carole and I had in a discreet corner of the dining room. A glass of brandy and a good cigar helped me to enjoy the cabaret, even though most of the singers had to rely on the new-style tonsil microphones to make their voices carry. I guess it's a sign of age, but I insist that *real* singers can get along perfectly well with the old type of mike they used to clip onto their back teeth. Still, considering how badly the day had started off, there was little to complain about. I had a glow of well-being, and Carole was looking incredibly feminine in something gauzy and golden. And in the bargain, I was earning money.

"When are you going to start earning your money?" Carole said, eyeing me severely through a small palisade of candle flames.

"I'm already doing it," I assured her, somewhat hurt by her attitude. "This is the hotel your father stayed in while he was in Milan, and there's a good chance this is where he made the connection. If it is, I'll pick up an echo sooner or later."

"Try to make it sooner, will you?"

"There's no controlling a wild talent." Sensing the need for more customer-relations work, I introduced a bit of echo chamber into my voice. "Right now, as we sit here, the intangible billowing nets of my mind are spreading outward, ever out . . ."

"Yes?"

"Hold on a minute," I said. Quite unexpectedly, the intangible billowing nets of my mind had caught a fish—in the shape of a passing wine waiter. He was a slim, dark youth with knowing brown eyes, and my psi faculties told me at once that his recent past was linked in some unusual way with that of Carole's father. I immediately tried to connect him with the "Mona Lisa" Mk. II. There was no positive response on the intuitive level, and yet I became more certain that the wine waiter would be worth questioning. That's the way ESP works.

Carole followed my gaze and shook her head. "I think you've had enough to drink."

"Nonsense—I can still crawl a straight line." I left the table and followed the waiter out through double doors and into a passageway, which probably led to the cellars. He glanced back when he heard me, then turned around, his eyes sizing me up like those of a cattle buyer examining a steer.

"Pardon me," I said. "Do you mind if I speak to you for a moment?"

"I haven't got a moment," he said. "Besides, I don't speak English."

"But . . ." I stared at him for a few seconds, baffled, then the message came through, loud and clear. I took out the expense money Carole had given me, peeled off a ten, and tucked it into the pocket of his white jacket. "Will that buy you a Linguaphone course?"

"It all comes back to me now." He smiled a tight, crafty smile. "You want a woman? What sort of woman do you want?"

"No. I do not want a woman."

He grew even more shifty-looking. "You mean . . . ?"

"I mean I've got a perfectly good woman with me."

"Ah! Do you want to *sell* a woman? Let me tell you, *signor,* you have come to the right man—I have many connections in the white slave market."

"I don't want to sell a woman, either."

"You are sure? As long as she has got white skin I can get you two thousand for her. It doesn't even matter," he said generously, jiggling cupped hands in front of his chest, "if she hasn't got much accouterments. As long as she has that flawless white skin . . ."

I began to get impatient. "All I want from you, Mario, is some information."

The gleam of avarice in the waiter's eyes was quickly replaced by a look of wariness. "How did you know my name?"

"I have ways of knowing things," I told him mysteriously. Actually, I wasn't sure whether I had esped his name or whether it was the only Italian one I could think of on the spur of the moment.

"Pissy," he said. "That's what you are—pissy."

I grabbed him by the lapels and raised him up on his toes. "Listen, Mario, any more lip out of you and I'll . . ."

"You've got me wrong, *signor,*" Mario babbled, and I was relieved to discover he was more of a coward than I am. "I mean, you are one of the pissy ones who know things without being told of them."

"P-S-I is pronounced like 'sigh,'" I said, letting go of his jacket. "Try to remember that, will you?"

"Of course, *signor.*" He stood back to let another waiter pass between us with a bottle of wine. "Now, tell me what information you want to buy, and I will tell you the cost. My scale of charges is very reasonable."

"But I've already paid you."

"No capisco," Mario said in a stony voice and began to walk away.

"Come back," I commanded. He kept on walking. I took out the roll of bills and he, displaying a sixth sense that aroused my professional envy, promptly went into reverse until we were facing each other again. It was as if he had been drawn toward me by a powerful magnet, and I began to realize that here was a man who was capable of selling his own grandmother. Indeed, from his earlier conversation, it was possible that he had already disposed of the old lady, venerable accouterments and all. Making a mental note to be careful in my dealings with Mario, I asked him if he could remember a Trevor J. Colvin staying at the hotel in April.

"I remember him," Mario nodded, but I could tell he was puzzled and slightly disappointed, which meant he had no idea of the money potentials involved. I decided to keep it that way.

"Why do you remember Mr. Colvin in particular? Had you any . . . ah . . . business dealings with him?"

"No—he didn't want a woman, either. All I did was introduce him to Crazy Julio from Paesinoperduto, my home village."

"Why was that?"

Mario shrugged. "*Signor* Colvin is an art dealer. Crazy Julio, who hasn't two lira to rub together, came to me with some ridiculous story about an old painting he had found on his farm. He wanted to show it to an art dealer, preferably one from another country. I knew it was a waste of time, but I'm a businessman, and if Crazy Julio was prepared to pay for my services . . ."

Wondering how much he knew of what had transpired, I said, "Did you perhaps translate for them?"

"No. Julio has English. Not very good English, though—he is too crazy for that."

"You didn't believe he had a painting that might be worth money?"

"Crazy Julio?" Mario sniggered into his hand. "His farm is just a patch of rock, and his only crop is empty Pepsi bottles."

"I see. Can you take me to him?"

Mario stopped sniggering on the instant, all his predatory instincts aroused. "Why do you want to see Crazy Julio?"

"The arrangement we have," I reminded him, "is that you answer my questions. Can you take me to him?"

Mario stuck out his hand. "A hundred dollars," he said peremptorily.

I touched his hand, trying to esp enough information to be able to proceed without him. All I could pick up was a blur of anonymous gray-green hillside strewn with boulders. The information I already had was enough to let me find Julio by working through a local inquiry agent, but that would use up extra time as well as money.

"Here's fifty on account," I said to Mario, slapping five bills into his palm. "When can we go?"

"Tomorrow morning I will borrow my mother's car and drive you to Paesinoperduto myself. How's that?"

"It suits me."

Mario gave a dry cough. "There will be a small extra charge for the use of the car. My mother is a widow, you understand, and hiring out the car my father left her is the only way she can afford a few little luxuries."

"That's all right." Wondering if I had been too harsh in my assessment of Mario's character, I arranged to meet him outside the hotel early the following day. I went back to the table and gave a glowing progress report to Carole. She was pleased enough to let us get onto first-name terms, but any hopes I had of further developments in the relationship were dashed when she insisted on our going to bed early, and separately, so that we would be fresh in the morning.

My room was cold and I slept rather badly, troubled by ominous dreams about a dark place and a strange wheel-like machine.

In the morning we waited outside the hotel for about ten minutes before Mario arrived to pick us up in a mud-spattered Fiat. It was my first time in Italy and, under the impression that Mediterranean countries were warm even in the winter, I had brought only a light showerproof. I was shivering violently in the raw wind while, in contrast, Carole looked rose-pink and competent in tweeds and fur. When Mario saw her the whites of his eyes flickered like the tallies of a cash register.

"*Three* thousand," he whispered to me as she got into the car. "That's the top rate around here."

I bundled him into the driver's seat and put my mouth close to his ear. "Keep quiet, you little toad. We Americans don't sell our women—besides, she doesn't belong to me."

Mario glanced again at Carole and then eyed me with surprise and contempt. "You are a great fool, *signor*. A woman like that cries out for love."

"You'll be the one who cries out if you don't shut up and start driving." I slammed the door on Mario, but he rolled down the window and held out his hand.

"Two hundred kilometers at twenty-five cents a kilometer makes fifty dollars," he said. "Payable in advance."

Seething with hatred, but trapped, I paid him the money and got in the back seat beside Carole. As the car moved off with a loud churning of dry gears, she drew her coat closer around her and gave me a cool stare.

"You're very generous with my money," she said. "I could have *bought* this heap for fifty dollars."

"Very funny." I huddled up in the opposite corner, numb with the cold, and brooded on the unfairness of life. Mario was a character straight out of a blue movie, but I had an uneasy feeling he might be right about Carole. Perhaps, in accordance with the whole blue movie ethos, she was sitting there, ice cold on the outside and burning hot within—a human antithesis to a Baked Alaska—just waiting for me to produce my dessert spoon and gobble her up. Perhaps, incredible as it seemed, she was a girl who longed to be dominated and ravished. I allowed myself a lingering glance at Carole's slim-sculpted legs and waited for her response.

"Keep your eyes on the scenery, junior," she snapped.

"That's what I was doing," I said weakly. Mario's shoulders twitched a little, and I guessed he was sniggering again. I began staring out the window, but the scenery was little consolation because we traveled only two blocks, went around a corner, and halted in the dimness of a shabby garage.

"Just a short delay, folks—I'll be with you in a minute," Mario called out. He leaped from the car, disappeared underneath it, and a few seconds later we heard a querulous whine, like that of a dentist's drill, coming up through the floor. I bore it for as long as I could, then got out and looked under the vehicle at Mario. He had disconnected its speedometer cable and was turning it with a power drill.

"Mario!" I bellowed. "What in hell do you think you're doing?"

"Just covering my expenses, *signor*."

"What do you mean?"

"I swore to my mother, on my honor, that we were only going twenty kilometers today, but I saw her taking a speedometer reading anyway." He began to sound aggrieved. "The old bitch doesn't even trust her own son! How do you like that? Every time I use her car I have to turn the speedo back or she would rob me blind."

I gave a strangled cry of fury, grabbed Mario by the ankles, and dragged him out from under the vehicle. "This is your last chance," I told him in a shaking voice. "Drive us to Paesino-whateveryoucallit right now, or the deal is off."

"All right. There's no need to get tough." Mario looked furtively around the garage. "By the way, now that you're at my depot—are you interested in drugs? Pot, hash, speed, snow. You name it, I've got it."

"Have you a telephone? I want to call the police."

The effect on Mario was gratifying and immediate. He pushed me back into the car and we drove off without even waiting to disconnect the power drill from the speedometer cable. It thumped on the bottom of the car a few times before falling behind us. Carole gave me a puzzled look, but I shook my head, warning her not to ask any questions.

All I knew for sure was that, if Mario got the slightest inkling of our business with Crazy Julio, he would move in like a hungry shark let loose in a paddling pool.

The drive westward into the first slopes of the Graian Alps was far from pleasant. There appeared to be no heater in the car and, for some reason known only to themselves, my nipples reacted to the cold by becoming unbearably painful. They were so hard they almost tore my shirt each time we lurched into a pothole. Carole was remote, wrapped in her plumage like a haughty bird. Even Mario had nothing to say, no criminal propositions to make. He drove with broody concentration, swerving every now and then in attempts to run over stray dogs. When we reached Paesinoperduto two hours after setting out, I felt like a very old man.

"Here we are," Mario announced, suddenly regaining his voice. "And I have a good idea."

"Yes?" I said warily.

"Crazy Julio's farm is two kilometers north of here, and the road gets even worse. You and the *signora* will stay here and have some coffee and I will bring Julio to meet you."

I shook my head. "Nothing doing, Mario. *You* are going to stay here while Miss Colvin and I drive to the farm by ourselves."

"That is impossible, *signor*. The car insurance would not cover you to drive it."

"The car hasn't even got insurance," I challenged.

"Also, you don't know the way."

"I can psi myself straight to it at this range."

"But do you think I could permit a stranger to drive off in my mother's car?"

"Let's see." I glanced around the deserted market square in which we had stopped. "I bet I can even psi the local police station from here."

"Be careful with the brakes," Mario said resignedly, getting out of the driver's seat and holding the door while I got in. "They pull to the right."

"Thanks." I let out the clutch pedal and steered the car toward the square's only northern exit.

"That was quite an exhibition," Carole said as we left the shabby cluster of dwellings behind. "Did you have to be so tough with that poor boy?"

"If that poor boy isn't in the Mafia," I assured her, "it's because they gave him a dishonorable discharge."

We drove along a deteriorating road, which took us up into the sunlit boulder-strewn hillsides I had psi-glimpsed on the previous evening. At one point—as if entering a baronial estate—the road crossed the remains of what had been a massive stone wall some centuries earlier. Faintly surprised at the idea of any medieval nobleman spending money on such unpromising land, I skried all around with a mounting sense of anticipation. There was a definite impression of richly appareled horsemen coming and going. When a track branched off to the right toward an isolated farmhouse clinging to the mountain, I knew at once that we had reached our destination. The car rocked violently on the stony ground, but I was too excited even to wince at the sawing of my nipples on the inside of my shirt.

"Is this it?" Carole's voice was full of doubt. "It doesn't look to me like a place where you'd pick up an original da Vinci."

"Me either—but I can tell you something big was going on here a few hundred years back." I stopped the car as it became in danger of being shaken to pieces. "Da Vinci spent a lot of his life in Milan, and it would have been quite easy for him to come up here in person any time he wanted."

"To that hovel?" Carole said scornfully, looking at the farmhouse ahead of us.

"It doesn't seem old enough. No, there's a cavern of some sorts around here, and that's probably where Julio found your painting." My heart speeded up as, once again, I glimpsed the circular wooden machine. This time I discerned something extra: There seemed to be a whole series of canvases arranged in a curving row. "I've a feeling there could be a lot more paintings in it."

Carole's gloved hand touched my shoulder. "You mean there's an underground storehouse?"

"I don't think that's the . . ." I stopped speaking as the figure of an elderly man emerged from the farmhouse and approached us. He was dressed in a pricey-looking chalk-striped gray suit, but the effect was spoiled by his frayed, collarless shirt and filthy tennis shoes. The double-barreled shotgun on his arm confirmed my opinion that he had very poor taste in separates.

I rolled down my window, projecting friendliness, and shouted, "Hi, Julio! How are you? How's it going?"

"What you want?" he demanded. "Go away."

"I'd like to talk to you."

Julio raised the shotgun. "I no want to talk to you."

"It's just for a few minutes, Julio."

"Listen, mister—I shoot you as soon as look at you." He scowled in the window at me. "In your case, sooner."

Stung by the insult, I decided on a more forceful approach. "It's about the 'Mona Lisa' you sold to *Signor* Colvin, Julio. I want to know where you got it, and you'd better tell me."

"I tell you nothing."

"Come on, Julio." I got out of the car and loomed over him. "Where is the cave?"

Julio's jaw sagged. "How you know about the cave?"

"I have ways of knowing things." I used quite a lot of echo chamber in the voice, aware that peasants tend to be afraid of espers.

Julio looked up at me with worried eyes. "I get it," he said in a low voice. "You are pissy."

"P-S-I is pronounced like 'sigh,'" I gritted. "Try to remember that, will you? Now, where's that cave?"

"You make trouble for me?"

"There'll be no trouble as long as you're a good boy, and there might even be some more money for you. The cave is this way, isn't it?" Following a powerful instinct, I began striding up the hillside toward a stand of dark-green trees. Julio jogged along at my side and Carole, who for once had nothing to say, left the car and came after us.

"I find it three-four year ago, but for long time I no touch," Julio said, panting a little as he struggled to keep abreast. "I no tell anybody because I want no fuss. Then I think: Why should I not have smart city clothes? Why should Crafty Mario be the only one to have smart city clothes? But I take only one picture to sell. Just one."

"How many paintings are in the cave?"

"Fifty. Maybe sixty."

I gave a short laugh. "Then it was pretty dumb of you to pick one as well known as the 'Mona Lisa.'"

Julio stopped jogging. "But, *signor*," he said, spreading his hands, "they are all 'Mona Lisas.'"

It was my turn to stop in my tracks. *"What?"*

"They are all 'Mona Lisas.'"

"You mean there are fifty or sixty paintings in there, and they're all the same?"

Julio shifted his feet uneasily. "They are not all same."

"This doesn't make sense." I glanced at Carole and saw she was equally baffled. "Come on—we've got to see this for ourselves."

By that time we had reached and entered the cluster of trees. Julio set his shotgun down, darted ahead of us, and dragged some pieces of rusty corrugated iron out of the way. Beneath them was an irregular opening and the beginning of a flight of stone steps, which led downward into blackness. Julio went down them, nimble in his tennis shoes, while Carole and I followed uncertainly. I felt her hand slip into mine and I gave it a reassuring squeeze as we reached the bottom step and began moving along what seemed to be a subterranean corridor. The daylight from the entrance rapidly faded.

I tapped Julio's shoulder. "How are we going to see? Have you got a flashlight?"

"Flashlight no good. I buy one with money *Signor* Colvin give me, but the crooks no tell me I have to keep on buying batteries. This is better." Julio struck a match and used it to light a storm lantern, which had been sitting on the stone floor. As the oil flame brightened I saw that the tunnel ended at a massive wooden door. Julio fumbled at the lock and pushed the door. In spite of its weight and great age, it swung open easily, with uncanny silence, and there was spacious darkness beyond. Carole moved closer to me. I put my arm around her, but at that moment I was too preoccupied to derive any enjoyment from the embrace—the mysterious chamber, at whose entrance we stood, contained the answers to all the questions that were pounding in my head. I could almost feel those cloaked figures from half a millennium in the past brushing by me, I could almost hear the master himself as he went secretly about his work, I could almost see the strange machine. The greatest genius of all time had left his imprint here, and his lingering presence was so overwhelming that ordinary mortals felt humbled and unwilling to intrude.

"What you wait for?" Julio snapped, marching into the chamber with the lantern held high.

I followed him and, in the shifting light, discerned the outlines of a circular wooden framework, which resembled a wheel lying on its side. It was large—perhaps twenty paces in diameter—and at its rim was as tall as a man. Beneath the spokes of the wheel was a dimly seen system of gears, with a long crankshaft running out to a position near where we stood. The whole thing reminded me of an early type of fun fair merry-go-round, except that in place of the carved horses—and difficult to see properly because of the intervening frames—there was a series of paintings. All of them were attached to the inside of the rim, facing the center. At the closest point on the machine's circumference there was a structure like an elaborately ornamented sentry box, on the rear wall of which were two small holes at eye level.

I gaped at the wheel for a moment while a fantastic concept struggled to be born in my mind. The device did look like a round-about, yet it had more in common with a Victorian cartoon animation machine. Realization exploded behind my eyes like a grenade.

Leonardo da Vinci—possessor of one of the most fertile minds in human history, creator of technologies that were far ahead of their times—had also invented moving pictures!

This machine, hidden for centuries in a cavern on a poor farmer's land, had to be the richest treasure ever to come out of antiquity. Beside it the tomb of Tutankhamen was a trifle, the Elgin marbles were reduced to insignificance—because the device itself was only one part of the incredible find. Where a lesser man would have experimented with the animation of simple drawings or silhouettes, Leonardo's towering vision and ambition had prompted him to aim for perfection, to base his work on his most acclaimed painting.

If my surmise was correct, the "Mona Lisa" was merely one frame in the world's first movie!

Hardly daring to breathe, I stepped into the viewing box and peered through the two holes. I had been right. Lenses concealed within the woodwork brought my gaze to a focus on yet another painting of the beautiful Florentinian lady. She looked startlingly real in the uncertain light, and in this picture her hands were in a much higher position, as if she were raising them to her throat. The famous smile seemed a little more pronounced, too. I had to step back to give myself time to assimilate what I had seen, and I noticed that Julio had hung his lantern on a hook projecting from the wall. He scuttled about, lighting other lanterns, then took hold of the long crankshaft in preparation for turning it.

"Does the mechanism still work?" I asked him.

Julio nodded. "I grease it and make it work." He wound the iron handle, and the framework began to turn. It moved very slowly at first, then settled into a smooth, noiseless rotation, which indicated perfection of balance. Julio gestured with his free hand, inviting me to look through the eyepiece again. He was grinning with proprietary glee.

I swallowed painfully as I stepped into the ornate box. Wonder was piling on wonder in a way that was almost too much to bear. On top of everything else that had transpired, I was about to have the privilege of actually viewing Leonardo's supreme masterpiece brought to magical life, to commune with his mind in a manner that nobody would have thought possible, to see his sublime artistry translated into movement. Perhaps I was even to learn the secret of the Gioconda smile.

Filled with reverence, I put my eyes to the viewing holes and saw the Mona Lisa miraculously moving, miraculously alive.

She raised her hands to the neckline of her dress and pulled it down to expose her ample left breast. She gave her shoulder a twitch, and the breast performed the classiest circular swing I had seen since the last night I witnessed Fabulous Fifi Lafleur windmilling her tassels in Schwartz's burlesque hall. She then drew her dress back up to its former position of modesty and demurely crossed one hand over the other, smiling a little.

"Oh, God," I whispered. "Oh, God, God, God, *God!*"

Julio kept cranking the machine, and I watched the show over and over again, unable to take my eyes away. It was a marvelous simulation of reality, marred only by one slight jerk near the beginning of the sequence—obviously where Julio had abstracted a painting to sell.

"Let me see it," Carole said, tugging at my sleeve. "I want to see it, too."

I stood back and let her look through the eyepiece. Julio twirled the crankshaft happily, jumping up and down in his tennis shoes like a demented dwarf. Carole viewed in silence for a full minute, then turned to me with wide eyes.

"It doesn't seem possible," she said faintly.

"Of course it's possible," I replied. "With a bit of practice some girls can do fantastic things with their accouterments. Why, I remember when Fabulous Fifi Lafleur used to . . ."

"I'm talking about da Vinci," Carole snapped. "I don't know

much about art, but I didn't think he would go in for that sort of thing."

"All artists are the same—they do whatever the paying customer wants them to do." I was speaking with newfound cynicism. "It's known that da Vinci was commissioned to design entertainments for various nobles, and some of the high-born were pretty low-minded."

"But all that work . . ."

"He probably had the assistance of a whole school of artists. Besides, a project this size accounts for the long periods of apparent unproductivity in da Vinci's career. When he should have been working on the Sforza statue he was down here working on Lisa's left . . ."

"Don't be vulgar," Carole put in. She turned back to the still-rotating machine. "How much do you think it's worth?"

"Who knows? Say there are sixty paintings involved. If they were smuggled out and away from the Italian Government they could fetch a million dollars each. Perhaps ten million each. Perhaps a billion—especially that one where she . . ."

"I *knew* this was going to be a lucky day," a familiar voice said from behind me.

I spun and saw Crafty Mario standing at the entrance to the chamber. He was holding the shotgun that Crazy Julio had dropped outside, and its barrels were pointing at my stomach.

"What do you want?" I demanded, and then—realizing just how rhetorical the question was in Mario's case—I added another: "Why are you pointing that gun at me?"

"Why did you steal my mother's car?" Mario gave one of his most unpleasant sniggers. "And why did you threaten me with the police?"

"You mustn't pay too much attention to the things I say."

"But I can't help it, *signor*—especially when I hear you saying things like 'sixty million dollars.' "

"Now, see here!" I started forward, but Mario stopped me by raising the shotgun.

"Yes?"

"We're being silly, with so much loot to go around. I mean, out of the sixty million you can have fifteen."

"I prefer to have sixty."

"But you wouldn't take a human life for an extra forty-five million, would you?" I looked into the polished pebbles that Mario used in place of eyes, and my spirits sank.

"Back against the wall, the three of you," Mario ordered.

Carole clung to me as we moved to the wall. Crazy Julio tried clinging to me as well, but I fended him off—with perhaps only a minute to live, I was entitled to be choosy.

"That's much better," Mario said. "Now, I will inspect the merchandise for myself."

He went toward the machine, which was still spinning on its well-greased bearings. Covering us with the gun, he stepped into the viewing box and peered into the two holes. I saw him stiffen with shock. He kept glancing back at us and then into the eyepiece again, fascinated. When he finally emerged from the box his face was almost luminescent with pallor. He walked toward us, his mouth working silently, and I held Carole close against me as we waited for the explosion of pain.

Mario appeared not to see us. He took the storm lantern down from its hook on the wall, and with a stiff-armed movement flung it into the center of the machine. There was a sound of breaking glass, then flames began to lick up around the dry timber structure.

"You fool!" I howled. "What are you doing?"

"You will see what I'm doing." Holding me in check with the gun, Mario collected the other lanterns and hurled them against the machine as well. The wooden rim of the wheel began to burn fiercely, and I knew that the paintings, my sixty "Mona Lisas," were igniting, crumbling, turning to worthless ash.

"You're mad," I shouted above the crackling of the flames. "You don't know what you've done."

"I know very well what I have done, *signor*," Mario said calmly. "I have destroyed a piece of pornographic filth."

"*You!*" I cackled like a madman. "But you're the most evil person I've ever known. You've robbed me since the minute we met, you rob your poor old mother, you tried to sell me a woman, you tried to buy Carole for the white slave trade, you're a drug pusher, and you were prepared to murder us a minute ago. You can't even drive a car without trying to run over cats and dogs."

"These things you say may be true, *signor*," Mario said with an odd kind of dignity, "but they do not prevent me from being a patriot. They do not prevent me from loving my glorious Italia."

"Huh? What the hell has patriotism got to do with it?"

"The great Leonardo was the finest artist who ever lived. He is the pride of my country—but tell me, *signor,* what would the rest of the world think of Italy if it was learned that the immortal Leonardo had prostituted himself in this way? What would they say about a nation whose noblest artist had wasted his divine gifts on . . ." Mario's voice quavered with anguish ". . . on medieval skin flicks?"

I shook my head, blinking back tears as the machine collapsed inward on itself in showers of topaz sparks. The chamber filled with smoke as the last fragments of the oil paintings were consumed.

Mario pointed to the exit. "All right—we can leave now."

"Aren't you going to shoot us?"

"It isn't necessary. Even if you were mad enough to talk about this, nobody would believe you."

"I think you're right." I gave Mario a curious stare. "Tell me, doesn't it bother you that you've just lost sixty million dollars?"

Mario shrugged. "Some days you win, some days you lose. By the way, because of all the trouble I've had, if you want to travel back to Milan in my mother's car there will be a small extra charge. . . ."

Carole stared at me thoughtfully as we sipped our after-dinner liqueurs. "You were very brave once or twice today—even with a gun pointed at you."

"It wasn't much. For all we know, Crazy Julio had no shells in it." I smiled at Carole across the candle flames. "I mean, he wouldn't even buy flashlight batteries."

"No, you were brave. I was quite impressed." Carole lapsed into another silence.

She had been like that all through the meal, even when I had pointed out that the painting she still had back in Los Angeles would make her a very rich woman. I guessed that the events of the day had been quite a strain on her, and that she was suffering from a reaction.

"It hardly seems possible," she said in a small voice.

I squeezed her hand. "Try to forget it. The main thing is that we got out of that cave in one . . ."

"I'm talking about the Mona Lisa," she interrupted. "That trick she did with her . . . um . . . accouterment. Do you think I could do it?"

I drained my brandy in one gulp. "I'm sure you could."

"Are you an expert on these things?"

"Well, I've seen Fabulous Fifi Lafleur a few times, and if she can do it you probably could."

"Let's go up to my room and find out," Carole said in a low, husky voice.

I tried to gulp more brandy from the empty glass and almost shattered it against my teeth. "You're kidding," I said, not very brilliantly.

"Do you think so?"

I looked at Carole, and something in her eyes told me she wasn't kidding. I'm too much of a gentleman to say anything about how the rest of that night worked out, but I'll tell you this much:

Every time I look at a copy of the "Mona Lisa," especially when I notice that famous smile, I can't help smiling back.

An Uncomic Book Horror Story

Frames 1 to 6:

Ahdnah crawled from the ruined shell of the escape capsule and took his first look at the world on which he was marooned. His reaction was one of intense disappointment. A sheet of glacial ice stretched from horizon to horizon, and the only movement was that of snow being whipped into flurries by the bitter wind.

There was no life here, and therefore there could be no food.

To a creature less superbly equipped for survival, the prospect would have meant certain death—but Ahdnah belonged to a talented and life-hungry species. He spent only a few seconds sorrowing over the fact that he would never again see his nest mother; then he began to dig.

The surface was hard and unyielding, but he altered his body, redesigning it to cope with the task before him. He transferred the metallic elements in his tissues to the lower side of his sluglike form, creating knife-sharp fins, which gouged through the black ice. Ahdnah quickly sank downward into a well of his own making, and by nightfall he had reached the inert soil of the planet itself. Here he discovered remains of vegetation compacted below the ice, and—reassured—continued burrowing to lower levels, far into the rock strata, where there were traces of residual heat.

When his instincts told him he had reached a safe depth, he halted and again changed the shape and nature of his body, this time choosing the minimum-surface-area configuration his people knew as the Sphere of Rest. That done, Ahdnah reduced his metabolism to its absolute minimum and sank into a mindless, dreamless sleep. The powdered ice in the well above him froze solid once more and was covered with drifting snow.

For a thousand years the glacier continued its march southward; then the climate relented, and the ice sheets began to retreat. They withdrew their sterile presence slowly and reluctantly, taking yet another three thousand years to uncover the entire extent of the plain under which Ahdnah lay buried. As the temperature increased, the levels of the seas rose and the shape of the land was changed. Forests spread everywhere, then were gradually destroyed by the activities of intelligent two-legged beings who arrived from more southerly regions to establish their civilization.

By that time even the tough metals of the survival capsule had surrendered to the forces of corrosion—but Ahdnah still lay in safety, far below the ground, sleeping and waiting.

Frames 7 to 17:

On almost any clear night on Ridgeway Street, especially if there was a moon, an open window could be seen at the top of the highest house. People out late sometimes saw a pale blur moving in the oblong of darkness and knew they had caught Willy Lucas watching them. And Willy, his pimply and fuzz-covered face twisted with panic, would lunge back from the window, afraid of being seen.

The women who lived opposite often thought that Willy was trying to spy into their bedrooms, and had had him punished by complaining to his brother. But Willy was not interested in the tight-lipped, bleak-eyed housewives of Ridgeway Street, nor in any woman outside those of his imagination. He simply enjoyed looking out across the silent town when all others had gone to sleep. It was as though they had died and left him alone, and there was nobody to shout at him or look at him with exasperation.

For this reason, on the rare occasions when he felt the need for exercise, he would usually go walking in the darkness, feeling contented and at ease in the deserted streets. At night the terraced dwellings seemed to have been drawn and filled in with India ink, and the windows, like those in his comic books, glowed a uniform yellow he found pleasing.

One sharp October night, when the moonlight lay in broad, frosty swathes across the rooftops, Willy was watching from his window and saw something climb out of the river, near the place where piles were being driven for a new warehouse. It was about the size of a man, but it moved with a curious leaden slowness that seemed inappropriate for someone who might have fallen into the chilly water.

Quivering with excitement, he snatched up his old mother-of-pearl opera glasses—stolen from Cooney's junk shop on the corner —and focused on the narrow strip of water visible between the houses where Ridgeway Street ran down to the river. The man, or animal, had vanished. Willy could see nothing but the disturbed surface of the water, each ripple limned with prismatic color by the damaged optical system of his glasses. Gradually the river returned to its former state of sentient smoothness, and it was as though nothing out of the ordinary had ever happened.

Willy watched until near dawn, crouched in the freezing darkness of his little attic; then he closed the window and went to bed.

When he woke up and came down for lunch, the greengrocery shop at the front of the house was crowded. His two sisters, Ada and Emily, were too busy to come back to prepare a meal for him, so Willy made sandwiches with mashed banana thickly smeared with marmalade. As he munched in silent abstraction he hardly saw the pages of the comic book he was leafing through or heard the sliding rumble of potatoes being weighed in the shop.

He was debating whether or not he should tell anybody about the strange event of the previous night. There was possibly a scandalous explanation for what he had seen—for instance, a neighbor falling into the river while going home drunk—in which case his sisters would have been interested. But after much consideration, Willy decided not to say anything. There had been the occasion when he had seen a highly respectable old lady from the next street steal a bunch of carrots from the shop. Willy, in an upsurge of family loyalty, had reported the incident to Ada and had been admonished for telling lies. Other, similar occurrences had made him wary when it came to communicating with his family.

He mooned around the house all day, going out only once, when he went to the river and wandered through the brambles and long grass, half expecting to find the body of a drowned man. He saw nothing and after a while became uneasy and went home, where his older brother—Jack—gave him an angry lecture about entering the house with muddy feet.

Frames 18 to 26:

That night, shortly after midnight, the thing came out of the water again.

It was difficult to see anything down at the water's edge—even the opera glasses did not help—but from his lofty vantage point Willy made out a segment of utter blackness moving slowly against the background of night. It remained at rest for some time, then moved out of sight behind the end houses. High up in his little room, Willy shivered with excitement.

He waited for a long time, straining his ears, and presently heard a faint, rhythmical thudding sound, which had a disturbing familiarity about it. The noise continued for several seconds and then stopped. Shortly afterward the black shape, still moving with painful slowness, reappeared and slipped down into the water.

When it had vanished, Willy pondered on what he had seen and heard, then went to bed, still unable to place the familiar sound. He dropped into a deep sleep.

The next day the customary bustle of Ridgeway Street was brought to a higher pitch than usual by the news of the disappearance of Des Martin. Martin was a taxi driver, a steady and industrious man, and one who was not likely to run out on his family. When the news reached Willy he recalled that Des Martin's way home lay along the riverbank. He also realized, belatedly, that the noise he had heard had been Martin pounding shut the sagging door of his rented garage.

Remembering the numerous occasions on which he had been thrown out of the taxi just for sitting in it while Des Martin was having a meal, Willy remained silent. Nobody would have paid attention to him anyway, even though Willy—with the alert instincts of one not altogether at home in the normal pattern of existence—knew that Des Martin had met the thing from the river.

Willy's principal reading matter since the torture of his schooldays had been horror comics. Indeed, he often wished he could live in a cartoon world, one in which all of life's difficulties could be resolved by the stroke of an artist's brush; in which everything was flat, simple, and brightly colored; and in which all sources of menace were clearly defined and understandable. He had always had an inner conviction that the night world contained many monsters, and he was, therefore, neither surprised nor distressed by his discovery that something alien and dangerous lived in the polluted waters of the river.

But there was one aspect of the affair that puzzled him: How he wondered, could such a slow-moving creature have gotten close enough to an active man like Des Martin to . . . to do whatever it had done? There was not much light down by the water's edge, yet it seemed strange that Des should have walked straight up to a ravenous beast, like a lamb to the slaughter, and allowed it to devour him.

The lurid, but limited, bestiary of Willy's imagination was unable to offer an immediate solution. He spent many hours speculating on the exact manner of Des Martin's death, occasionally chuckling as a particularly satisfying vision crossed his mind.

Frames 27 to 38:

Two days had gone by, and things were returning to normal when—late at night—Willy saw the dark shape make its next appearance. As before, it emerged from the water with the slowness of a garden slug, remained motionless for several seconds, and then passed out of sight.

An hour, then two hours, ticked by in the chilly silence of the attic, and Willy began to think that the chances of anybody coming along were remote. Suddenly he heard, from the next street, echoing up through the nighttime stillness, the sharp, ringing sound of high heels on the pavement. Willy frowned for a moment until his torpid brain, in which were stored detailed timetables for almost everyone in the district, came up with an identification.

The wearer of the noisy shoes had to be Jane Dubois, who worked in the coffee bar up on the main road. She was only a waitress there, but she had taken it on herself from time to time to refuse admittance to Willy, even when he had money. The rapid clicking of her heels grew louder, then began to fade away again as Jane went down the hill toward the river.

Quite suddenly her footsteps ceased.

Willy listened carefully, but there was no sound of a front door being dragged shut. And he knew that the thing from the river was feeding.

He continued his vigil until, some time afterward, the patch of creeping blackness returned to the waters. He closed his window and lay down, smiling in the darkness—the taste of revenge had none of the bitterness caused by the guilt of personal participation. The only thing marring his contentment was the nagging curiosity about how the dark horror caught its prey. Jane Dubois was young and agile, yet she had been taken—instantaneously, it seemed—in a well-lit street. Was it possible that the monster could make itself invisible?

Willy turned the problem over and over in the dim recesses of his mind until he fell asleep.

Frames 39 to 56:

The second disappearance caused a greater commotion than the first, and people began to stay off the streets late at night. Willy did not miss them and, even if he had, there were police patrol cars that swished past the house every now and then to provide him with something to watch. He would have been quite happy if there had been no people on the streets—ever.

On the third night after Jane's disappearance, Willy's friend—which was how he was coming to think of the entity in the river—went hungry. It came out of the river around midnight, as usual, and flowed out of Willy's field of view. The streets were deathly quiet, and Willy sensed at once that no victims would be abroad. A vague unease began to build in his mind. The thing returned to the water just before dawn, and came out earlier that night—only to be disappointed once more. Willy began to worry.

When Willy was absent-minded it reduced him to a state of near imbecility. Once, while hanging around the shop, he knocked over a basket of tomatoes, and another time dropped a crate of empty Coca-Cola bottles on the tiled floor. Jack came home from work just as Willy was brushing up the broken glass, and Jack shouted for a full five minutes. Willy stared down at his brother's angry oil-stained face and stocky denim-clad figure. Willy did not say anything, but he wished that Jack would go for a walk down by the river late at night. He began to wonder if there might be some way to get Jack to go out at the right time and in the right direction.

That night the creature came out earlier than on any previous occasion, and Willy knew it was becoming very hungry. He watched and waited all night, but nobody came, and in the darkness of predawn the thing reappeared on the river's edge on the way back to its lair. Somehow Willy could *feel* its anger and disappointment and hunger, as though the creature were a part of himself. He leaned out of the window, straining his eyes, wishing he could think of a way to help his friend. Suddenly he froze.

The shape had paused on the edge of the water and, although he could discern only a black patch in the darkness, he knew it had seen *him*. In some way, alien to humans, it had become very much aware of Willy—and it dawned on him that the mysterious entity was not his friend at all.

It began to inch its way up Ridgeway Street.

Willy fell back from the window in terror. High up above the street he had imagined himself safe, but he had no idea what powers the thing might have. It might be able to climb a vertical wall. Willy had a vision of a black monster, hideous jaws agape, bursting in through his window. Or it might, like some horrors he had seen in his comics, be able to exert telepathic control over him and make him go down the stairs and out into the street.

All at once there was a burst of sound and a flash of light outside. Willy moaned in panic, then realized it was a police car going by. He returned to the window and looked out. The car had swung off into one of the smaller streets that branched off Ridgeway and, down at the river, only a few ripples catching the first light of dawn showed that anything had ever been there.

Frames 57 to 63:

Even in the brightness of morning, Willy remained afraid. That one instant of mental contact with the alien horror had burned itself far into his mind and had changed his whole outlook. He would have to tell somebody what he knew.

This presented a whole series of problems.

The first time he had seen the thing he had decided it would be pointless to try making people believe him—and that had been before the two disappearances. The story he had to tell now was so fantastic that he would receive greater derision, or greater punishment, than ever.

He was brooding on the situation over breakfast when Ada and Emily came into the kitchen with instructions from Jack that he was to spend the day painting the walls of the yard at the back of the shop. Willy shambled out, lay down in the dusty shed where the potato sacks were stored, and thought hard about what he might do. Finally, he decided to write an anonymous letter to the police—that way he would receive more credibility and still remain out of trouble.

He slipped upstairs to his room, where he managed to find some reasonably clean sheets of paper. The letter took him several hours. In it he told the events of the past days as clearly and simply as he could, covering four sheets with his ungainly scrawl. After much deliberation he signed himself, "A Well-wisher."

It was late in the afternoon before the letter was sealed in an envelope, and then Willy remembered he needed a stamp. He hung around the shop until there was a lull in business, and Ada and Emily went into the kitchen to prepare a meal for Jack coming home from work. Willy took a stamp from the till and went upstairs for his coat. When he came down Jack was waiting for him with an intense, furious look on his square face, his eyes narrowed to slits.

Six speech balloons:

"Take your coat off," Jack snapped. "Get out to the back and finish that job, or you get nothing to eat."

Willy gaped at him—he had forgotten the whitewashing. "Ah . . . I'm not hungry. I don't want nothin' to eat."

"That's your business. But you're going to paint the yard anyway."

"But I've got to . . ."

"To what?"

"Nothin'," Willy said sullenly.

Frames 64 to 81:

Willy turned and hurried through the house, taking his coat off as he went. Outside in the yard he attacked the whitewashing with a ferocity that surprised his family, splashing the liquid on to the uneven bricks in long, curving strokes, heedless of his clothes. Two hours later the job was done, and Willy, aching and blistered, seized his coat. As he was going out through the kitchen, Jack tried to make him sit down and eat, but Willy—his round face shiny with sweat—brushed on past him.

Outside in Ridgeway Street he stopped with a jerk. It was dark!

It was dark, the street was empty, and—down toward the river—the blackness seemed to be alive and crawling with menace.

Willy considered going back into the security of the house. But then the letter would not be posted till the next day, and the police would not receive it until the day after that—which might be too late. Taking a deep, shuddering breath, Willy ran up the hill away from the river and turned right onto the main road, where he sped along trying to remember the whereabouts of the nearest post office.

Suddenly he saw a pillar box in the darkness of the first street on his right, the one that ran parallel to Ridgeway. With a grateful whimper he pulled the crumpled letter from his pocket, loped up to the pillar box, and pushed it in.

Too late he remembered that he had never seen a pillar box there before.

Too late it occurred to him that a really fearsome comic book monster might be able to change its shape, to make itself look like anything it wanted.

And, much too late, he felt the hot breath issuing from the oblong mouth, as it closed greedily on his wrist.

Deflation 2001

Having to pay ten dollars for a cup of coffee shook Lester Perry.

The price had been stabilized at eight dollars for almost a month, and he had begun to entertain an irrational hope that it would stay there. He stared sadly at the vending machine as the dark liquid gurgled into a plastic cup. His expression of gloom became more pronounced when he raised the cup to his lips.

"Ten dollars," he said. "And when you get it, it's cold!"

His pilot, Boyd Dunhill, shrugged, then examined the gold braid of his uniform in case he had marred its splendor with the unaccustomed movement of his shoulders. "What do you expect?" he replied indifferently. "The airport authorities refused the Coffee Machine Maintenance Workers' pay claim last week, so the union told its members to work to rule, and that has forced up the costs."

"But they got 100 per cent four weeks ago! That's when coffee went up to eight dollars."

"The union's original claim was for 200 per cent."

"But how could the airport pay 200 per cent, for God's sake?"

"The Chocolate Machine Workers got it," Dunhill commented.

"Did they?" Perry shook his head in bewilderment. "Was that on television?"

"There hasn't been any television for three months," the pilot reminded him. "The technicians' claim for a basic two million a year is still being disputed."

Perry drained his coffee cup and threw it into a bin. "Is my plane ready? Can we go now?"

"It's been ready for four hours."

"Then why are we hanging around here?"

"The Light Aircraft Engineers' productivity agreement—there's a statutory minimum of eight hours allowed for all maintenance jobs."

"Eight hours to replace a wiper blade!" Perry laughed shakily. "And that's a productivity deal?"

"It has doubled the number of man-hours logged at this field."

"Of course it has, if they're putting down eight hours for half-hour jobs. But that's a completely false . . ." Perry stopped speaking as he saw the growing coldness on his pilot's face. He remembered, just in time, that there was a current pay dispute between the Flying Employers' Association and the Low-wing Twin-engined Private Airplane Pilots' Union. The employers were offering 75 per cent and the pilots were holding out for 150 per cent, plus a mileage bonus. "Can you get a porter to carry my bag?"

Dunhill shook his head. "You'll have to carry it yourself. They're on strike since last Friday."

"Why?"

"Too many people were carrying their own bags."

"Oh!" Perry lifted his case and took it out across the tarmac to the waiting aircraft. He strapped himself into one of the five passenger seats, reached for a magazine to read during the flight to Denver, and then recalled that there had been no newspapers or magazines for over two weeks. The preliminaries of getting airborne took an unusually long time—suggesting that the air traffic controllers were engaged in some kind of collective bargaining—and finally Perry drifted into an uneasy sleep.

He was shocked into wakefulness by a sound of rushing air, which told him that the door of the aircraft had been opened in flight. Physically and mentally chilled, he opened his eyes and saw Dunhill standing at the yawning door. His expensive uniform was pulled into peculiar shapes by the harness of a parachute.

"What . . . what is this?" Perry said. "Are we on fire?"

"No." Dunhill was using his best official voice. "I'm on strike."

"You're kidding!"

"You think so? I just got word on the radio—the employers have turned down the very reasonable demands of the Low-wing Twin-engined Private Airplane Pilots' Union and walked out on the negotiations. We've got the backing of our friends in the Low-wing Single-engined and in the High-wing Twin-engined unions; consequently all our members are withdrawing their labor at midnight, which is about thirty seconds from now."

"But, *Boyd!* I've no 'chute—what'll happen to me?"

A look of sullen determination appeared on the pilot's face. "Why should I worry about you? You weren't very concerned about me when I was trying to get along on a bare three million a year."

"I was selfish. I see that now, and I'm sorry." Perry unstrapped himself and stood up. "Don't jump, Boyd—I'll double your salary."

"That," Dunhill said impatiently, "is less than our union is claiming."

"Oh! Well, I'll triple it then. Three times your present salary, Boyd."

"Sorry. No piecemeal settlements. They weaken union solidarity." He turned away and dived into the roaring blackness beyond the doorway.

Perry stared after him for a moment, then wrestled the door shut and went forward to the cockpit. The aircraft was flying steadily on autopilot. Perry sat down in the left-hand seat and gripped the control column, casting his mind back several decades to his days as a fighter pilot in Vietnam. Landing the aircraft himself would get him in serious trouble with the unions for strikebreaking, but he was not prepared to die just yet. He disengaged the autopilot and began to get in some much-needed flying practice.

Some thousands of feet below the aircraft, Boyd Dunhill pulled the ripcord and waited for his 'chute to open. The jolt, when it came, was less severe than he had expected, and a few seconds later he was falling at the same speed as before. He looked upward and saw—instead of a taut canopy—a fluttering bunch of unconnected nylon segments.

And, too late, he remembered the threat of the Parachute

Stitchers and Packers' Union to carry out disruptive action in support of their demand for longer vacations.

"Communists!" he screamed. "You lousy Red anarchist ba . . ."

CRUNCH!

Waltz of the Bodysnatchers

"I think I can be of service to you," the pale stranger said. "I want to commit suicide."

Lorimer looked up from his drink in surprise. Even in the half light of the bar, it was obvious that the dull-voiced man who had come to his table was ill, shabby, and tired. His thin shoulders were bowed within his cloak, making him appear as slight as a woman, and his eyes smoldered with broody desperation in a white, triangular face. *What a wreck!* Lorimer thought contemptuously. *What a pitiful bloody mess!*

"I said, 'I want to commit suicide,'" the stranger repeated, his voice louder but still lifeless.

"Don't shout it all over the place." Lorimer glanced around the cavernlike bar and was relieved to see that there was nobody within hearing distance. "Sit down."

"All right." The man sagged into a chair and sat with his head lowered.

Looking at him, Lorimer began to feel a furtive, pounding elation. "Do you want a drink?"

"If you're buying, I'll have one; if you're not, I won't. It doesn't really matter."

"I'll get you a beer." Lorimer pressed the appropriate button on the order display, and a few seconds later a beaker of dark ale emerged from the table's dispensing turret. The stranger seemed not to notice, and Lorimer pushed the cool ceramic over to him. He drank from it without relish, automatic as the machine that had served him.

"What's your name?" Lorimer said.

"Does it matter?"

"To me, as a person, it doesn't matter a damn—but it's more

convenient when everybody has a label. Besides, I'll need to know all about you."

"Raymond Settle."

"Who sent you, Raymond?"

"I don't know his name. A waiter down at Fidelio's. The one with the rosewood hair."

"Rosewood?"

"Brown, with black streaks."

"Oh." Lorimer recognized the description of one of his most trusted contacts, and his sense of elation grew stronger. He stared at Settle, wondering how any man could let himself get into such a leached-out state. Something about the way Settle spoke suggested he was intelligent and well-educated, but—Lorimer drew comfort from the thought—intellectuals were usually the ones who folded up when the going got a little tough. For all their so-called brains, they never seemed to learn that strength of body led to strength of mind.

"Tell me, Raymond," he said, "what relatives have you got?"

"Relatives?" Settle stared down at his drink. "Just one. A baby girl."

"Is that who you want the money to go to?"

"Yes. My wife died last year, and the baby is in Our Lady of Mercy's Hostel." Settle's lips stretched in what ought to have been a smile. "Apparently I'm considered unfit to bring her up by myself. The Office of the Primate would overlook my various character defects if I had money, but I'm not equipped to earn money. Not in the conventional manner, anyway."

"I see. Do you want me to set up a trust fund for the kid?"

"That's about the best thing I could leave her."

Lorimer felt an uncharacteristic chill of unease, which he tried to ignore. "Just our luck to be born on Oregonia, eh?"

"I don't know much about luck."

"I mean, life's a lot simpler on planets like Avalon, Morgania, or even Earth."

"Death's a lot simpler, too."

"Yeah, well . . ." Lorimer decided to keep the conversation businesslike. "I'll have to get more details from you. I'm paying twenty thousand monits, and I have to be sure nothing goes wrong."

"No need to apologize, Mr. Lorimer. I'll tell you anything you want to know." Settle spoke with the calm disinterest of one whose life had already ended.

Lorimer ordered another drink for himself, making a determined effort not to become contaminated by the other man's despair. The important and positive thing to concentrate on was the fact that Settle—in dying—would open up rich new lives for two other human beings.

The next morning the double suns were close together above the eastern horizon, merging into an elongated patch of brilliance that imprinted peanut-shaped afterimages on the retina. Lorimer floated up from the city through flamboyant forests of gold shading into tan. On the crest of the hill, surrounded by vistas of complicated shoreline and small islands, he steered his skimmer off the road and allowed it to sink to the ground in the gardens of the Willen house. He got out of the vehicle, stood for a moment, appreciating the luxury of his surroundings, then walked the short distance to the patio at the rear of the house.

Fay Willen was seated on a bench with her back to him, busy stretching canvas over a wooden frame. She was wearing a simple white dress, which enhanced the lustrous blackness of her hair. Lorimer paused again, drinking in the vision of what was his already by natural law and what was soon to come into his legal possession. He made a sound with his feet, and Fay whirled to face him, startled.

"Mike!" she said, getting to her feet. "What are you doing here so early?"

"I had to see you."

Fay frowned a little. "Wasn't that a little risky? You didn't even call to check if Gerard was still away."

"It doesn't matter."

"But he's bound to get suspicious if you . . ."

"Fay, I told you it doesn't matter." Lorimer was unable to suppress the triumph in his voice. "I found one."

"You found what?" Fay was still displeased, unwilling to relax or warm to him.

"The thing you said I'd never find in a hundred years—a man who wants to commit suicide."

"Oh!" The small hammer she had been holding clattered on the patio with a curious ringing sound. "Mike, I never thought . . ."

"It's all right, sweetie." Lorimer took Fay in his arms and was surprised to feel that she was trembling. He held her tightly, remembering all the times he had gotten his way in disagreements simply by making her aware of the pent-up strength in his body.

"You won't even have to be there when it happens," he murmured. "I'll take care of everything."

"But I never really expected to be mixed up in a murder."

Lorimer experienced a flicker of impatience but was careful not to reveal it. "Listen, sweetie, we've been over all this before. We won't be *murdering* Gerard—we'll just be dispossessing him."

"No, I don't like it." Fay looked up at him with troubled eyes.

"Just dispossessing him, that's all," Lorimer coaxed. "It isn't your fault that the Church and the law somehow got rolled into one on this planet. On any other world you'd be able to get a divorce for the things Gerard has done—or on account of what he doesn't do—but here the system forces you to take other steps. They don't even permit emigration. It's the system's fault, not yours."

Fay disengaged herself from his arms and sat down again. Her oval face had lost its color. "I know Gerard is old. I know he's cold . . . but, no matter what you say, he'd still have to be killed."

"It doesn't even have to hurt him, for God's sake—I'll get a cloud gun for the job." The meeting with Fay was not working out as Lorimer had planned it, and he could feel his self-control slipping. "I mean, how long would he be clinically dead? Just a couple of days in an open-and-shut case like the one we're planning."

"It isn't right, Mike."

"As far as Gerard would know, he would close his eyes and wake up in a different body." Lorimer sought for ways to strengthen his argument. "A *younger* body, too. This guy I've got lined up doesn't seem very old. We would even be doing Gerard a favor."

Fay hesitated, then slowly shook her head, with fixed eyes, as though following the sweep of a massive pendulum. "I've decided against it. If I agreed before, it was only because I thought it could never happen."

"You're making this difficult for me," Lorimer said. "I can't really believe you've changed your mind. I mean, if you had, I'd almost be tempted to blackmail you into it—for your own good."

Fay gave a short laugh. "You couldn't blackmail me."

"I could, Fay, believe me. The Primate doesn't like anybody to engage in adultery, but I'm just a man—with a tendency to venal sin built into him—and I'm not married. I'd probably get a month's suspended sentence. You, on the other hand, are a woman who has betrayed a faithful husband. . . ."

"Gerard *has* to be faithful! He isn't equipped for anything else."

"The Primate won't hold that against him. No, sweetie, all the money and fancy lawyers in the world wouldn't save you from going up for a year. At least a year." Lorimer was relieved to see that Fay looked suitably horrified. She had the advantages of being rich and beautiful, but when it came to emotional or intellectual in-fighting a certain passivity in her nature guaranteed him victory every time. He paused for a few seconds, long enough to let the threat of prison have maximum effect; then he straddled the bench beside Fay.

"You know, this is the craziest conversation I've ever heard," he said soothingly. "Why are we talking about blackmail and prison when we could be talking about our future together? You hadn't really changed your mind, had you?"

Fay stared at him in sad speculation. "No, Mike. Not really."

"That's great—because this character I found yesterday is too good to waste." Lorimer squeezed Fay's hand. "It turns out he's an unsuccessful artist. I thought you could sell anything in the art line these days, but if there were any garrets on Oregonia this guy would be starving in one of them. That reminds me, can you let me have the payoff money now?"

"Twenty thousand, wasn't it?"

"Yes."

"I think there's more than that in the downstairs safe. I'll get it for you now." Fay turned to leave, then paused. "What's his name?"

"Raymond Settle. Have you heard of him?"

Fay shook her head. "What sort of paintings does he do?"

"I don't know." Lorimer was slightly taken aback by the question. "Who cares, anyway? The only thing that matters is that he's determined to kill himself."

On the way back down the gilded hill and into town, Lorimer reviewed his plan. Its elements were simple. Gerard Willen was an industrious and moderately successful businessman, so nobody could really say he had married Fay for her money. He had seen her once, had fallen in love, and had courted her with a desperate ardor to which Fay—always liable to manipulation by anyone with strong motivations—had easily succumbed. The trouble with their marriage was that Gerard, as though having expended the dregs of his vitality on the chase, had almost immediately become paternal rather than passionate. He demanded no more of Fay than that she be seen on his arm at Church functions and formal dinners.

The biological pressures had built up within Fay for more than a year, and Lorimer—fencing coach at an exclusive gymnasium—counted himself lucky to have appeared on the scene at precisely the right time to act as a release mechanism.

In the beginning, for about a month, he had been content just to possess Fay's body; then had come the conviction that he had earned all the things that went with it. He wanted the money, the splendid houses, the status, and—above all—the escape from the hopeless daily chore of trying to impart grace to plump matrons who used their foils like fly swatters. But Gerard Willen stood squarely in the way.

On Earth, or one of fifty other planets, there would have been the twin possibilities of divorce or straightforward murder. On Oregonia, neither of these options was open. The dominance of the Mother Church meant that divorce was impossible, except in very extreme circumstances. It was certainly out of the question for a minor thing like sexual incompatibility. And murder—due to the fact that Oregonian law prescribed Personality Compensation as a punishment—was much too risky.

It was dark when Lorimer parked his floater at the prearranged meeting point on the northern outskirts of the city. For an uneasy moment he thought Settle had failed to make it; then he noticed the thin figure emerging from the blackness of a clump of trees. Settle was moving slowly, weaving a little, and he had difficulty in getting into the vehicle.

"Have you been drinking?" Lorimer demanded, scanning the dimly seen triangular face.

"Drinking?" Settle shook his head. "No, my friend, I'm hungry. Just hungry."

"I'd better get you something to eat."

"That's very kind of you, but . . ."

"I'm not being kind," Lorimer interrupted, unable to conceal his disgust. "It would ruin the whole thing if you died on us. I mean, if your body died."

"It won't," Settle told him. "It hangs onto life with a tenacity I find a little disconcerting—that's my whole problem, after all."

"Whatever you say." Lorimer boosted the floater up off the ground and drove it forward. "We can't afford to be seen together, so keep your head down. I'm taking you up to the Willen house."

"Are we going to do it tonight?" A rare note of animation had crept into Settle's voice.

"No. Gerard Willen is still out of town, but you'll have to see the layout of the place in advance, to make sure nothing goes wrong on the big night."

"I see." Settle sounded disappointed. He tightened his cloak around himself, huddled down in the passenger seat, and remained quiet for the rest of the journey up to the house. Lorimer did not mind the silence—talking to the other man made him feel cold and, in a way he failed to understand, threatened. He made his way up the hill, choosing roads he knew would be deserted, and parked in the lee of the big house. The night air felt crisp as he stepped out of the floater, and the starlight lay like an unseasonal frost on the lawns and hedges. They went through to the patio at the back, where yellow radiance from the windows of the house provided enough illumination for them to see clearly. Lorimer took the cloud gun from his pocket and handed it to Settle, who gripped it with a thin, reluctant hand.

"I thought you said it wasn't tonight," Settle whispered.

"Just get used to the feel of the gun—we can't afford for you to miss." Lorimer urged his companion forward. "The plan is that you're supposed to be sneaking into the house to steal something—the fact that you're a down-and-out will make the story sound even better. You go in through this french window, which is never locked, and you start looking around for valuables." Lorimer turned the handle of the window frame and pushed it open. Warm air billowed around them as they went inside the long, unlit room.

"What you don't know is that right next to this room is Gerard Willen's study, where he has a habit of working late at night, when he should be in bed with his wife. You move around in here for a while, then you knock something over. This would do." Lorimer pointed at a tall vase on a shelf.

"Willen hears the noise, and comes in through that door over there. You panic and smoke him a couple of times with your gun. Do it as many times as you want—just make sure he dies."

"I've never killed anybody," Settle said doubtfully.

Lorimer sighed. "You're not killing him—you're killing yourself. Remember?"

"I guess so."

"Don't forget it. When Willen goes down, you stand looking at him—stupefied—until Fay Willen appears in the doorway. You let her get a good look at you, then you throw the gun down and make a run for it, back out the way you came in. The police pick you up in less than an hour. Fay identifies you. You confess. And that's it!"

"I didn't realize it would be so complicated."

"It's *simple,* I tell you." The hopeless monotone of Settle's voice had angered Lorimer to the point where he felt like throwing a punch. "Nothing could be easier."

"I don't know . . ."

Lorimer gripped Settle's shoulder and was appalled at how frail it felt beneath the cloak. "Listen, Raymond, you want your kid to get the money, don't you? Well, this is the only way you can fix it."

"What will happen to me . . . afterward? Will it hurt?"

"The experts say it's absolutely painless." Lorimer poured

warm encouragement into his voice, clinching his victory. "There'll be a very brief trial, possibly on the same day, and you'll be found guilty. All they'll do then is put a kind of helmet over your head and another one on Willen's head. They'll plug you both into the cerebral coupler, throw a switch, and it will all be over."

"I'll be gone forever?"

"That's right, Raymond. The transfer process takes about a millionth of a second—so there isn't time to feel pain. You couldn't get a better way out." Lorimer spoke convincingly, but in his heart there were doubts. Advanced neuro-electronics had made it possible to punish a killer—and, to a large extent, recompense the victim—by transferring the mind of the dead person into the body of the murderer. It was a neat, logical system; but, if it was as humane as its proponents claimed, why was it not practiced universally? Why was Personality Compensation banned on a number of progressive worlds?

Lorimer decided not to distract himself with needless speculation. All he had to remember was that displacement of identity was one of the very few grounds upon which the Oregonian Mother Church would grant a divorce. Gerard Willen would live on in Settle's body—but, because it was a body different from the one that had mouthed the holy vows and shared Fay's matrimonial bed, the marriage would automatically be terminated. Lorimer thought it ironic that the Church, which regarded a marriage as an eternal union of souls, should be so anxious to dissolve the bond at the first hint of physical promiscuity. *If it suits His Holiness,* he thought, returning his attention to the matter at hand, *it suits me.* He went over the plan twice more with Settle, rehearsing him carefully for his part, ducking out of the way each time the inexperienced Settle allowed the gun to swing in his direction.

"Watch where you're pointing that thing," he snapped. "Try to remember it's a lethal weapon."

"But you wouldn't be dead—you'd only be displaced," Settle said. "They'd put your mind into my body."

"I'd rather stay dead." Lorimer stared at Settle in the dimness of the room, wondering if there had been a hint of amusement or malice in his last remark. "You'd better give the gun back to me before there's an accident."

Settle compliantly handed the weapon over, and Lorimer was in the act of dropping it into his pocket when the door to the room was thrown open. Lorimer spun, instinctively leveling the gun at the figure in the lighted doorway; then he saw that the intruder was Fay. His forehead beaded with sweat as he realized he had almost been startled into pulling the trigger.

"Mike? Are you there?" Fay turned on the room lights and stood blinking in the sudden brilliance.

"You bloody little *fool!*" Lorimer snarled. "I told you to stay upstairs if you heard anybody in here tonight."

"I wanted to see you."

"You nearly got yourself smoked! You nearly . . ." Lorimer's voice failed him as he thought of what might have happened.

"I'm in on this thing, too," Fay said unconcernedly. "Besides, I wanted to meet Mr. Settle."

Lorimer shook his head. "It's better that you don't. The less previous association there is, the less chance of somebody being able to prove collusion."

"There's nobody in the house but the three of us." Fay looked past him at Settle. "Hello, Mr. Settle."

"Mrs. Willen." Settle gave an absurdly dignified bow, his eyes fixed on Fay's face.

Lorimer became aware that Fay was wearing a rather unsubstantial black nightdress, and he felt a surprising pang of annoyance. "Go back upstairs," he said. "Raymond and I were just about to leave. Isn't that right, Raymond?"

"That is correct." Settle smiled, but his face was paler and more desperate than ever. He swayed slightly and caught a chairback for support.

Fay started forward. "Are you ill?"

"It's nothing to be concerned about," Settle replied. "I seem to have forgotten to eat anything for a couple of days. Careless of me, I know . . ."

"You must have something before you leave."

"I offered him a meal, but he turned it down," Lorimer put in. "He doesn't like eating."

Fay gave him a look of exasperation. "Bring Mr. Settle through to the kitchen. He's going to have some milk and hot steak sandwiches." She strode ahead of them, switched on the sonic oven, and in little more than a minute had served Settle with a liter of cold milk and a platter of aromatic toasted sandwiches. Settle nodded his gratitude, untied his cloak, and began to eat. Watching him devour the food under Fay's approving gaze, Lorimer got a feeling that in some obscure way he had been cheated. He developed an inner conviction that if Fay had not been present Settle would have continued refusing to eat, which seemed to indicate that he was now playing for sympathy.

When the realization came to him that he was beginning to consider Settle as a rival for Fay's affections, Lorimer gave a low chuckle. If there was one thing he knew for certain about Fay it was that—after Gerard Willen—she had no room in her life for yet another tired, thin, and sickly man. He moved over beside Fay and put his arm around her shoulders, holding her securely within the aura of his own physical strength. He watched Settle with a kind of proprietary amusement.

"Look at him eat," he whispered. "I told you he was a starving artist."

Fay nodded. "I wonder why he wants to die."

"Some people let themselves get that way." Lorimer decided against mentioning the existence of Settle's daughter, in case it made Fay go soft. "If you ask me, it's the best thing for him."

A few minutes later Settle raised his eyes from the empty platter. "I would like to thank you for the . . ." His words faded away, and he sat staring at something on the opposite side of the large room. Lorimer looked in the same direction, but could see nothing there except for one of Fay's meaningless paintings, incomplete and still on the easel, which she must have dragged in from the patio and forgotten to put away.

Settle looked at her and said, "Is this your work?"

"Yes, but I'm sure it won't mean anything to you."

"It looks to me as though you were painting light itself. With no containment. With no reference whatsoever to restrictive masses."

Lorimer began to laugh, then he felt Fay make an involuntary movement. "That's right," she said quickly, "but how did you know? Have you tried the same thing?"

Settle gave a sad, hopeless smile. "I wouldn't have the courage."

"But surely . . ."

"Let's break this up," Lorimer said impatiently. "Raymond has been here too long already, and if somebody sees him the whole plan is wiped out."

"How could anybody see him?" Fay said.

"An unexpected visitor could drop in."

"At this time of night?"

"Or somebody could call you on the seephone."

"That's hardly likely, Mike. I can't think why anybody in the . . ." Fay had been speaking with a firmness that Lorimer found slightly disconcerting, but she allowed the sentence to tail off uncertainly as the kitchen filled with a gentle chiming. It was the call signal from the seephone in the corner.

"I'd better see who it is." Fay spoke in a low voice as she moved toward the screen.

"Wait till we get out of here," Lorimer said urgently, feeling his nerves vibrate in time with the insistent signal.

"It's all right—I'm accepting the call in sound only." Fay touched a button on the communications console, and the image of Gerard Willen appeared on the screen. He was a frail-looking man in his fifties, with a long serious face and pursed mouth, and dressed in somber business clothes.

"Hello, Gerard," Fay said. "I wasn't expecting a call from you."

"Fay?" Willen's eyes narrowed as he peered at his own screen. "Why can't I see you, Fay?"

"I'm getting ready to go to bed, and I'm not properly dressed."

Willen nodded his approval. "You are wise to be careful—I've heard of godless individuals who intercept domestic calls in the hope they will be able to practice voyeurism."

Fay gave an audible sigh. "The Devil is always learning new tricks. Why did you call me, Gerard?"

"I have good news. I have completed my business in Holy Cross City and will be flying out tomorrow morning. That means I shall be with you before noon."

"I'm so glad." Fay shot Lorimer a significant glance. "You've been away too long."

"I am looking forward to being back," Willen said in his precise, neutral tones. "I have a difficult report to write and will be able to concentrate much better in the peace of my own study."

That's what you think, Lorimer chanted to himself, feeling an upsurge of confidence and joy. He listened intently to the rest of the conversation, despising Willen and at the same time feeling grateful to him for not displaying a single sign of warmth, for not uttering even one word that could give Fay cause to imagine that the relationship might be redeemed. Settle, too, was sitting upright at the table, watching Fay and the image of her husband with an attentiveness that contrasted with his former apathy. His deep-set eyes looked feverish and, again, Lorimer found himself wishing that Fay was wearing a less revealing garment. As soon as the call had ended and the screen had gone blank, Lorimer went to Fay and caught both her hands in his.

"This is it, sweetheart," he said. "Everything's falling into place for us."

"Ah . . . I'm afraid not," Settle put in unexpectedly.

Lorimer turned on him. "What are you talking about?"

Settle's face was haggard, but when he spoke, his voice was strangely resolute. "I've been thinking the whole thing over while I was watching Mr. Willen on the screen, and I've realized I can't go through with it. In spite of all the things you say about merely displacing his personality, I could never make myself shoot another human being.

"I'm afraid there's no way you can talk me into it."

Several times, as he waited in the near darkness beyond the patio, Lorimer took out the cloud gun and checked it over. It was one of the most perfect killing machines ever devised, but so much was depending on it that he was unable to resist examining its settings again and again. Settle stood impassively beside him, unmoving, his black-cloaked figure like something carved in obsidian. Above their heads, a tiny greenish moon threaded its way among thickets of stars.

The hours had passed slowly, and it was close to midnight when the light from a window in the upper part of the house abruptly faded. Lorimer's heart began to beat faster, and his gloved palms grew moist.

"Fay's gone to bed," he whispered. "We'll be able to move in soon."

"Ready when you are."

"I'm glad to hear it." As the final minutes dragged by, Lorimer felt relieved that his period of dependence on the unstable and unpredictable Settle would soon be over. Settle's announcement, on the previous night, that he would be unable to shoot Willen had seemed like the end of everything. Lorimer had experienced a few unpleasant moments until it had been established that Settle was still prepared to fulfill most of his bargain. He was prepared to accept the blame for the shooting and to yield his life for it, as long as somebody else actually pulled the trigger. Lorimer was far from happy with the modified plan, because it involved his being at the scene of the crime instead of establishing an alibi elsewhere, but he had learned that it was difficult to coerce a determined suicide. There was simply no leverage. Given time, he might have been able to work something out, but an instinct was telling him it would be a bad thing to give Fay and the artist the chance to develop an association. It was better to press ahead, regardless of minor imperfections in the scheme.

"Come on—we've waited long enough," Lorimer said. He moved onto the patio, walking as quietly as possible to avoid disturbing Willen prematurely. It was vital that the shooting should take place under cover of the darkness within the house so that Willen would not recognize his attacker and—after being restored to life in Settle's body—give evidence to the police. With Settle close behind him, Lorimer avoided the pool of mellow light issuing from the window of Willen's study. He reached the french windows of the adjoining room, went inside, and drew Settle in after him by the arm.

"You stand right here by the window," Lorimer said. "If Gerard sees anything when he opens the door, we want it to be you."

He took a large ceramic vase from a shelf, then crouched down behind a chair, holding the vase in his left hand and the cloud gun

in his right. It occurred to Lorimer that he should wait a few minutes to let his eyes grow accustomed to the near blackness, but
now that the time had come, he was tense and impatient. He
lobbed the vase into the air, and it shattered against the opposite
wall.

The suddenness of the sound was almost explosive. There was a
moment of ringing silence, then a muffled exclamation filtered
through from the next room.

Lorimer aimed the gun at the door and tightened his finger on
the trigger. There were footsteps outside in the corridor. The door
was flung open, and Lorimer—in the same instant—squeezed the
trigger. Once, twice, three times.

Three clouds of immediate-acting toxin hissed through the
clothing and skin of the vague figure silhouetted in the doorway,
each a guarantee of instantaneous death, and a split-second later
the room lights came on. Lorimer cowered back under the shock
of the unexpected brilliance, his eyes staring.

Gerard Willen stood motionless in the doorway, hand on the
light switch, gazing at Lorimer with a look of pure astonishment
on his long face.

Lorimer leaped to his feet, terrified, instinctively leveling the
gun. Gerard Willen lurched toward him, but there was no accom-
panying movement of his feet. He toppled forward, his face
smashed into the corner of a low table with a pulpy sound, and he
slumped sideways onto the floor. He had died so quickly that his
body had been taken by surprise.

"Oh, Christ," Lorimer quavered, "that was awful!"

He found himself staring down at the gun in his hand, awed by
its powers; then his sense of purpose and urgency returned. Every
citizen of Oregonia had to wear a biometer implanted under the
skin of his left shoulder, and Willen's—reacting to the cessation of
bodily functions—would be broadcasting an alarm signal. The fact
that there had been no medical symptoms prior to the death would
be regarded by the computer at Biometer Central as a circum-
stance worthy of investigation. Lorimer calculated that it would be
less than five minutes until an ambulance and a police vessel
floated down onto the lawns of the Willen house. He turned to Set-

tle, who was staring fixedly at the body on the floor, and handed him the gun. Settle accepted the weapon with trembling hands.

"Don't let it throw you," Lorimer said.

"I can't help it—look at his face."

"It isn't worrying him. Concentrate on what you have to do next. As soon as Fay comes in that door and screams, you throw down the gun and get the hell out of here. Go out the front way and down Ocean Drive. The street lights are good out there, so somebody's bound to see you. With any luck the police could spot you from the air. Okay?"

"Okay."

"When that happens, all your troubles will be over."

Settle nodded. "I know it."

"Listen, Raymond . . ." Something about the way the other man had spoken, about the way he was so ready to accept death, aroused Lorimer's compassion. He touched Settle awkwardly on the shoulder. ". . . I'm sorry about the way things worked out for you."

"Don't worry about me, Mike." Settle managed a brief, wistful smile.

Lorimer nodded and, aware that he had wasted enough time, turned and ran toward his skimmer. As he left the patio and sped across the grass, a woman's scream echoed behind him, and he knew the plan was being completed right on schedule. He located the skimmer, jumped in, and slammed the canopy down. The vehicle lifted responsively and, without turning on his lights, Lorimer accelerated away from the house. He drove inland on full boost, flitting among the trees like a night-flying bird, invisible in the darkness, until he reached a secondary road several kilometers from the coast.

The road was free of traffic, as Lorimer had expected. He reduced power and brought the skimmer down to the regulation traffic height of one meter, then turned on his lights and flew toward the city at a moderate and unremarkable speed. As the distance markers slipped by in soothing progression, the tension that had been causing the gnawing sensation in his stomach began to abate.

There had been a certain amount of risk, but it had been worth taking. All he had to do now was remain discreetly in the background until Settle was convicted and Gerard Willen's identity was transferred into his body. Divorce under those circumstances was always rushed through by the Office of the Primate in a matter of days, and then Lorimer would be able to step forward and claim his prize—or, rather, his multiplicity of prizes. There was Fay herself, the three houses, the money, the status . . .

By the time Lorimer reached the apartment building where he lived, he was almost drunk with happiness. He drove his skimmer up the ramp, grounded it with a flourish, and rode up to his apartment in the elevator tube. In the privacy of his own rooms, he stood for a moment savoring the sheer pleasure of being alive, then poured himself a tall drink. He was raising it to his lips when the door chimes sounded. Lorimer carried his drink to the door, sipping it as he walked. He opened the door, saw two grim-faced men standing on the threshold, and a stab of anxiety pierced his euphoria.

"Michael T. Lorimer?" one of the men said.

Lorimer nodded cautiously. "What of it?"

"Police. You're under arrest. We're taking you to Police Central."

"That's what you think," Lorimer said, with automatic defiance, and began to back away.

The man who had spoken to him glanced at his companion and said, "Don't take any chances with him."

"Right." The companion raised his hand, and Lorimer glimpsed the flared snout of a bolas gun. Without hesitation, the policeman fired the weapon, and a weighted ribbon of metal wrapped itself around Lorimer's shins, solidifying into an unbreakable bond in less than a second. Another shot hit him in the chest, pinning his arms to his sides. Deprived of all power of movement, he overbalanced and would have gone down had the two men not caught him. They dragged him to the elevator tube and took him down to a large skimmer and lifted him inside. One of them slipped into the driver's seat, and Lorimer fought to control his panic as the vehicle surged toward the exit ramp.

"You're making one hell of a mistake," he said, forcing his

voice to sound both angry and confident. "What am I supposed to have done?"

Neither of the men answered, and Lorimer guessed they had no intention of speaking to him, no matter what he said. He watched the route the vehicle was taking, until he was certain they really were heading for Police Central; then he turned his attention to the problem of what he ought to do next. Something had gone wrong—that much was only too obvious. But what? The only thing he could think of was that Settle had been picked up very quickly and, at the last minute, had funked making a confession. The obvious thing for him to do then would be to accuse Lorimer of the killing.

Lorimer forced himself to think calmly about the situation, and felt a growing conviction that he had hit on the truth. Settle's weakness and instability had been adverse factors all along, and it would be in character for him to back away from the final, decisive step that would lead to his death. It was just what one would expect from an ineffectual suicidal type, but—Lorimer felt an upsurge of optimism—Settle was backing a loser. His fingerprints, not Lorimer's, were on the murder weapon, and he had entered the house in a manner that was an indictment in itself. Those two circumstances were damning enough, but the blackest mark against him was that Fay would not corroborate his story. It was the word of a shabby down-and-out against the combined testimonies of a rich and respected woman and a citizen who had never been in any previous trouble.

In a few minutes of ghosting through quiet streets, the skimmer reached Police Central and came to rest in the entrance bay. One of the men snipped the coil away from Lorimer's legs, making it possible for him to get out of the vehicle with reasonable dignity, but they left his arms strapped to his sides. Inside the brightly lit building a number of people glanced curiously at Lorimer and, while he was being bundled into the elevator tube, he began rehearsing his lines. An air of injured innocence would, he decided, be more effective than loud indignation. Perhaps a tone of mild reproach and a hint of reluctance to consider suing for wrongful arrest . . .

When he was led into an office to face three officials in the blue collarettes of inspectors, Lorimer was fully composed and almost looking forward to the contest of wits.

"Perhaps one of you gentlemen will explain what's going on here," he said, meeting their eyes unflinchingly. "I'm not accustomed to his sort of thing."

"Michael Thomas Lorimer." The senior inspector of the three spoke in a careful voice while glancing at a compcard in his hand. "I am charging you with the murder of Gerard Avon Willen."

"Gerard Willen? *Dead?*" Lorimer looked shocked. "I can't believe it."

"Have you anything to say in reply to the charge?"

"Who would want to . . . ?" Lorimer paused for a moment, as though he had just comprehended the inspector's opening statement. "Wait a minute—you can't charge *me* with murder. I didn't know anything about it. I haven't been near the Willen place for weeks."

"We have a witness."

Lorimer gave a comfortable laugh. "I'd like to know who he is."

"The principal witness is not a man. Mrs. Willen has testified that she saw you shoot her husband and run from the house."

The floor seemed to heave beneath Lorimer's feet. "I don't believe you," he said.

One of the other inspectors shrugged and held up a recorder. On its small screen there appeared an image of Fay, her cheeks glistening with tears, and Lorimer heard her say the words that condemned him. *I've been had,* he thought strickenly, as a dark flood of understanding welled in his mind. *The bitch has decided to drop ME!* Awareness of his peril jolted Lorimer's brain into desperate activity.

"This is a big shock for me," he said urgently, "but I think I can explain why Mrs. Willen told you a lie like that."

"Proceed." There was a flicker of interest in the senior inspector's eyes.

"You see, I got to know Mrs. Willen when I was teaching her to fence. We got to talking quite a bit, and she invited me up to her house a few times. I thought she was just being normally friendly—

so you can imagine the way I felt when I realized she wanted me to have an affair with her."

"How did you feel, Mr. Lorimer?"

"Disgusted, of course," Lorimer said with maximum candor. "She's an attractive woman and I'm only human, but I draw the line at adultery. When I turned her offer down she seemed to go insane for a few minutes—I've never seen anybody so angry. She said things I don't like to repeat."

"Under the circumstances, I think you should put your scruples aside."

Lorimer hesitated. "Well, she said she would get out of her marriage to Gerard Willen somehow, no matter what it took. And she said she'd make me sorry for the way I'd treated her. I never thought anything like this would come out of it . . ." Lorimer gave a shaky laugh ". . . but now I'm beginning to understand that old saying about a woman scorned."

"You tell an interesting story, Mr. Lorimer." The senior inspector examined his fingernails for a moment. "Have you ever met a man called Raymond Settle?"

"I don't think so."

"That's odd. He was at the Willen house tonight, and he too says he saw you shoot Mr. Willen."

"*What?* But why should I kill Gerard?"

"There's a sum of twenty thousand monits in cash missing from the wall safe in the room where Willen was killed. Money we recovered from your apartment tonight. Settle says he was in the study with Willen when they heard a sound in the next room. Settle says that Willen went to investigate and . . ."

"That's ridiculous," Lorimer shouted. "Who *is* this man Settle, anyway? He must be in on it with Fay—they must have cooked this up between them. That's it, Inspector! He must be Fay Willen's latest boyfriend. He must have sneaked into the house . . ." Lorimer stopped speaking as he saw that the inspector was shaking his head.

"It won't do, Mr. Lorimer." The inspector's voice was almost kind. "Raymond Settle was a trusted business associate of Mr. Willen, and a friend of the family for many years. He had every right to visit Gerard Willen this evening."

Lorimer opened his mouth to argue, then closed it without uttering a sound. Wordless—and helpless—he was just beginning to appreciate the full extent of what had been done to him.

Exactly a year later, three people attended a discreet celebration in the many-mirrored dining room of the large house overlooking the sea.

Gerard Willen, clothed in the flesh that had once belonged to a young and ambitious fencing coach, poured three glasses of imported champagne. As he did so, he took pleasure in the easy strength and steadiness of the hand in which he held the dewed bottle. It was an enjoyment that never seemed to fade.

"You know," he remarked, "this is a superb body I have . . . inherited. It was a pity that friend Lorimer didn't have the mental equipment to match."

Raymond Settle shook his head. He was as gaunt as ever, but when freshly groomed and expensively clad, his tall frame appeared wiry rather than frail. His left arm was around Fay's waist, and she had nestled contentedly against his side.

"It was lucky for us that Lorimer wasn't too bright," he said. "I thought I was going to laugh and give the game away when I was feeding him that mush about a baby daughter in an orphanage."

Fay smiled up at him. "You were very good, Raymond. Very convincing."

"Perhaps—though sometimes I feel a bit guilty about it—we played him like a fish."

"Forget it. The man was a murderer." Willen handed around the beaded glasses and raised his own. "Here's to me!"

"Why not to all of us?" Fay said.

Willen smiled. "Because I got the most out of it. You escaped from a marriage you were tired of, but I wanted the divorce, too—and in the bargain I got a new physique, which lets me work twenty hours a day if I feel like it."

"You always did work too much," Fay told him.

Willen looked thoughtful. "I suppose the old me must have been rather boring."

"Not rather boring. *Very* boring."

"I think I deserve that. Mind you . . ." Willen glanced appreciatively at Fay ". . . the new me could be different. Now that I've got the hormone production of a young stallion, I've realized there are more enjoyable pursuits than work."

"How interesting!" Fay detached herself from Settle, laughing, and moved closer to Willen with an exaggerated sway of her hips. "Perhaps you'll come around and see me some time—when Raymond's not here, of course."

"Cut that out, you two," Settle protested with a good-natured grin. "You're beginning to worry me."

"Don't be silly, darling." Fay smiled at him over the rim of her champagne glass. "Here's to the sanctity of marriage."

"I'll drink to that." Settle drained his glass, and then—when he noticed that Fay and Willen were gazing at him with amused expectancy—began to wonder if his drink had tasted exactly the way champagne should.

A Little Night Flying

The dead cop came drifting in toward the Birmingham control zone at a height of some three thousand meters. It was a winter night, and the subzero temperatures that prevailed at that altitude had solidified his limbs, encrusted the entire body with black frost. Blood flowing through shattered armor had frozen into the semblance of a crab, with its claws encircling his chest. The body, which was in an upright position, rocked gently on stray currents, performing a strange aerial shuffle. And at its waist a pea-sized crimson light blinked on and off, on and off, its radiance gradually fading under a thickening coat of ice.

Air Police Sergeant Robert Hasson felt more exhausted and edgy than he would have felt after an eight-hour crosswind patrol. He had been in the headquarters block since lunchtime, dictating and signing reports, completing forms, trying to wrest from the cashier's office the expenses that had been due to him two months earlier. And then, just as he was about to go home in disgust, he had been summoned to Captain Nunn's office for yet another confrontation over the Welwyn Angels case. The four on remand—Joe Sullivan, Flick Bugatti, Denny Johnston, and Toddy Thoms—were sitting together at one side of the office, still in their flying gear.

"I'll tell you what disturbs me most about this whole affair," Bunny Ormerod, the senior barrister, was saying with practiced concern. "It is the utter indifference of the police. It is the callousness with which the tragic death of a child is accepted by the arresting officers." Ormerod moved closer to the four Angels, protectively, identifying with them. "One would think it was an everyday occurrence."

Hasson shrugged. "It is, practically."

Ormerod allowed his jaw to sag, and he turned so that the brooch recorder on his silk blouse was pointing straight at Hasson. "Would you care to repeat that statement?"

Hasson stared directly into the recorder's watchful iris. "Practically every day, or every night, some moron straps on a CG harness, goes flying around at five or six hundred kilometers an hour, thinking he's Superman, and runs into a pylon or a towerblock. And you're dead right—I don't give a damn when they smear themselves over the sides of buildings." Hasson could see Nunn becoming agitated behind his expanse of desk, but he pressed on doggedly. "It's only when they smash into other people that I get worked up. And then I go after them."

"You hunt them down."

"That's what I do."

"The way you hunted down these children."

Hasson examined the Angels coldly. "I don't see any children. The youngest in that gang is sixteen."

Ormerod directed a compassionate smile toward the four black-clad Angels. "We live in a complex and difficult world, Sergeant. Sixteen years isn't a very long time for a youngster to get to know his way around it."

"Balls," Hasson commented. He looked at the Angels again and pointed at a heavy-set, bearded youth who was sitting behind the others. "You—Toddy—come over here."

Toddy's eyes shuttled briefly. "What for?"

"I want to show Mr. Ormerod your badges."

"Naw. Don't want to," Toddy said smugly. " 'Sides, I like it better over here."

Hasson sighed, walked to the group, caught hold of Toddy's lapel, and walked back to Ormerod as if he were holding nothing but the piece of simulated leather. Behind him he heard frantic swearing and the sound of chairs falling over as Toddy was dragged through the protective screen of his companions. The opportunity to express his feelings in action, no matter how limited, gave Hasson a therapeutic satisfaction.

Nunn half rose to his feet. "What do you think you're doing, Sergeant?"

Hasson ignored him, addressing himself to Ormerod. "See this badge? The big *F* with wings on it? Do you know what it means?"

"I'm more interested in what your extraordinary behavior means." One of Ormerod's hands was purposely, but with every appearance of accident, blocking his recorder's field of view. Hasson knew that this was because of recent legislation under which the courts refused to consider any recorded evidence unless the entire spool was presented—and Ormerod did not want a shot of the badge.

"Have a look at it." Hasson repeated his description of the badge for the benefit of the soundtrack. "It means that this quote child unquote has had sexual intercourse in free fall. And he's proud of it. Aren't you, Toddy?"

"Mr. Ormerod?" Toddy's eyes were fixed pleadingly on the barrister's face.

"For your own good, Sergeant, I think you should let go of my client," Ormerod said. His slim hand was still hovering in front of the recorder.

"Certainly." Hasson snatched the recorder, plucking a hole in Ormerod's blouse as he did so, and held the little instrument in front of the Angel's array of badges. After a moment he pushed Toddy away from him and gave the recorder back to Ormerod with a flourish of mock courtesy.

"That was a mistake, Hasson." Ormerod's aristocratic features had begun to show genuine anger. "You've made it obvious that you are taking part in a personal vendetta against my client."

Hasson laughed. "Toddy isn't your client. You were hired by Joe Sullivan's old man to get him out from under a manslaughter charge, and big, simple Toddy just happens to be in the same bag."

Joe Sullivan, sitting in the center of the other three Angels, opened his mouth to retort, but changed his mind. He appeared to have been better rehearsed than his companions.

"That's right," Hasson said to him. "Remember what you were told, Joe—let the hired mouth do all the talking." Sullivan shifted resentfully, staring down at his blue-knuckled hands, and remained silent.

"It's obvious we aren't achieving anything," Ormerod said to Nunn. "I'm going to hold a private conference with my clients."

"Do that," Hasson put in. "Tell them to peel off those badges, won't you? Next time I might pick out an even better one." He waited impassively while Ormerod and two policemen ushered the four Angels out of the room.

"I don't understand you," Nunn said as soon as they were alone. "Exactly what did you think you were doing just now? That boy has only to testify that you manhandled him . . ."

" 'That boy,' as you call him, knows where we could find the Fireman. They all do."

"You're being too hard on them."

"You aren't." Hasson knew at once that he had gone too far, but he was too obstinate to begin retracting the words.

"What do you mean?" Nunn's mouth compressed, making him look womanly but nonetheless dangerous.

"Why do I have to talk to that load of scruff up here in your office? What's wrong with the interview rooms downstairs? Or are they only for thugs who haven't got Sullivan money behind them?"

"Are you saying I've taken Sullivan's money?"

Hasson thought for a moment. "I don't believe you'd do that, but you let it make a difference. I tell you those four have flown with the Fireman. If I could be left alone for half an hour with any one of them I'd . . ."

"You'd get yourself put away. You don't seem to understand the way things are, Hasson. You're a skycop—and that means the public doesn't want you around. A hundred years ago motorists disliked traffic cops for making them obey a few common-sense rules; now everybody can fly, better than the birds, and they find this same breed of cop up there with them, spoiling it for them, and they *hate* you."

"I'm not worried."

"I don't think you're worried about police work either, Hasson. Not really. I'd say you're hooked on cloud-running every bit as much as this mythical Fireman, but you want to play a different game."

Hasson became anxious, aware that Nunn was leading up to something important. "The Fireman is real—I've seen him."

"Whether he is or not, I'm grounding you."

"You can't do that," Hasson blurted instinctively.

Nunn looked interested. "Why not?"

"Because . . ." Hasson was striving for the right words, any words, when the communicator sphere on Nunn's desk lit up redly, signaling a top-priority message.

"Go ahead," Nunn said to the sphere.

"Sir, we're picking up an automatic distress call," it replied with a male voice. "Somebody drifting out of control at three thousand meters. We think it must be Inglis."

"Dead?"

"We've interrogated his compack, sir. No reponse."

"I see. Wait till the rush hour is over and send somebody up for him. I'll want a full report."

"Yes, sir."

"I'm going up for him now," Hasson said, moving toward the door.

"You can't go through the traffic streams at this hour." Nunn got to his feet and came around the desk. "And you're grounded. I mean that, Hasson."

Hasson paused, knowing that he had already stretched to the limit the special indulgence granted to members of the Air Patrol. "If that's Lloyd Inglis up there, I'm going up to get him right now. And if he's dead, I'm grounding myself. Permanently. Okay?"

Nunn shook his head uncertainly. "Do you want to kill yourself?"

"Perhaps." Hasson closed the door and ran toward the tackle room.

He lifted off from the roof of the police headquarters into a sky that was ablaze with converging rivers of fire. Work-weary commuters pouring up from the south represented most of the traffic, but there were lesser tributaries flowing from many points of the compass into the vast aerial whirlpool of the Birmingham control zone. The shoulder lights and ankle lights of thousands upon thousands of fliers shifted and shimmered, changes of parallax causing spurious waves to progress and retrogress along the glowing streams. Vertical columns of brilliance kept the opposing elements apart, creating an appearance of strict order. Hasson knew, however, that the appearance was to some extent deceptive. People who were in a hurry tended to switch off their lights to avoid detection and fly straight to where they were going, regardless of the air corridors. The chances of colliding with another illegal traveler were vanishingly small, they told themselves, but it was not only occasional salesmen late for appointments who flew wild. There were the drunks and the druggies, the antisocial, the careless, the suicidal, the thrill seekers, the criminal—a whole spectrum of types who were unready for the responsibilities of personal flight, in whose hands a countergravity harness could become an instrument of death.

Hasson set his police flare units at maximum intensity. He climbed cautiously, dye gun at the ready, until the lights of the city were spread out below him in endless glowing geometries. When the information display projected onto the inner surface of his visor told him he was at a height of two hundred meters, he began paying particular attention to his radar. This was the altitude at which rogue fliers were most numerous. He continued rising steadily, controlling the unease that was a normal reaction to being suspended in a darkness from which, at any moment, other beings could come hurtling toward him at lethal velocity. The aerial river of travelers was now visible as separate laminae, uppermost levels moving fastest, which slipped over each other like luminous gauze.

A farther eight hundred meters and Hasson began to relax slightly. He was turning his attention to the problem of homing in on Inglis when his proximity alarm sounded and the helmet radar flashed a bearing. Hasson twisted to face the indicated direction. The figure of a man flying without lights, angled for maximum speed, materialized in the light of Hasson's flare units. Veteran of a thousand such encounters, Hasson had time to calculate a miss distance of about ten meters. Within the fraction of a second available to him, he aimed his gun and fired off a cloud of indelible dye. The other man passed through it—glimpse of pale, elated face and dark, unseeing eyes—and was gone in a noisy flurry of turbulence. Hasson called headquarters and gave details of the incident, adding his opinion that the rogue flier was also guilty of drug abuse. With upward of a million people airborne in the sector at that very moment, it was unlikely that the offender would ever be caught, but his flying clothes and equipment had been permanently branded and would have to be replaced at considerable expense.

At three thousand meters Hasson switched to height maintenance power, took a direction-finder reading on Inglis's beacon, and began a slow horizontal cruise, eyes probing the darkness ahead. His flares illuminated a thickening mist, placing him at the center of a sphere of foggy radiance and making it difficult to see anything beyond. This was close to the limit for personal flying without special heaters, and Hasson became aware of the cold that was pressing in on him, searching for a weakness in his defenses. The traffic streams far below looked warm and safe.

A few minutes later, Hasson's radar picked up an object straight ahead. He drew closer until, by flarelight, he could make out the figure of Lloyd Inglis performing its grotesque shuffle through the currents of dark air. Hasson knew at once that his friend was dead, but he circled the body, keeping just outside field interference distance, until he could see the gaping hole in Inglis's chest plate. The wound looked as though it had been inflicted by a lance.

A week earlier, Hasson and Inglis had been on routine patrol over Bedford when they had detected a pack of about eight flying without lights. Inglis had loosed off a miniflare, which burst just beyond the group, throwing them briefly into silhouette, and both men had glimpsed the slim outline of a lance. The transportation of *any* solid object by a person using a CG harness was illegal, because of the danger to other air travelers and people on the ground, and the carrying of weapons was rare even among rogue fliers. It seemed likely that they had chanced on the Fireman. Spreading their nets and snares, Hasson and Inglis had flown in pursuit. During the subsequent low-level chase, two people had died—one of them a young woman, also flying without lights, who had strayed into a head-on collision with one of the gang. The other had been a pack leader who had almost cut himself in two on a radio mast. At the end of it, all the two policemen had had to show for their efforts had been four unimportant members of the Welwyn Angels. The Fireman, the lance carrier, had gotten away to brood about the incident, safe in his anonymity.

Now, as he studied the frozen body of his former partner, Hasson understood that the Fireman had been inspired to revenge. His targets would have been identified for him in the news coverage given to the arrest of Joe Sullivan. Swearing in his bitterness and grief, Hasson tilted his body, creating a horizontal component in the lift force exerted by his CG harness. He swooped in on the rigid corpse, locked his arms around it and, immediately, both bodies began to drop as their countergravity fields canceled each other out. No stranger to free fall, Hasson efficiently attached a line to an eye on Inglis's belt and pushed the dead man away from him. As the two separated to beyond field interference distance, the upward rush of air around them gradually ceased. Hasson checked his data display and saw that he had fallen little more than a hundred meters. He paid the line out from a dispenser at his waist until Inglis's body was at a convenient towing distance, then he flew west, aiming for a point at which it would be safe to descend through the commuter levels. Far beneath him the traffic of the Birmingham control zone swirled like a golden galaxy, but Hasson—at the center of his own spherical universe of white, misty light—was isolated from it, cocooned in his own thoughts.

Lloyd Inglis—the beer-drinking, book-loving spendthrift—was dead. And before him there had been Singleton, Larmor, and McMeekin. Half of Hasson's original squad of seven years ago had died in the course of duty—and for what? It was impossible to police a human race that had been given its three-dimensional freedom with the advent of the CG harness. Putting a judo hold on gravity, turning the Earth's own attractive force back against itself, had proved to be the only way to fly. It was easy, inexpensive, exhilarating—and impossible to regulate. There were eighty million personal fliers in Britain alone, each one a superman impatient of any curb on his ability to follow the sunset around the curve of the world. Aircraft had vanished from the skies almost overnight, not because the cargo-carrying ability was no longer needed, but because it was too dangerous to fly them in a medium that was crowded with aerial jaywalkers. The nocturnal rogue flier, the dark Icarus, was the folk hero of the age. What, Hasson asked himself, was the point in being a skycop? Perhaps the whole concept of policing, of being responsible for others, was no longer valid. Perhaps the inevitable price of freedom was a slow rain of broken bodies drifting to Earth as their powerpacks faded and . . .

The attack took Hasson by surprise.

It came so quickly that the proximity alarm and the howling of air displaced by the attacker's body were virtually simultaneous. Hasson turned, saw the black lance, jackknifed to escape it, received a ferocious glancing blow, and was sent spinning—all in the space of a second. The drop caused by the momentary field interference had been negligible. He switched off his flares and flight lights in a reflexive action and struggled to free his arms from the towline, which was being lapped around him by his own rotation. When he had managed to stabilize himself he remained perfectly still and tried to assess the situation. His right hip was throbbing painfully from the impact, but as far as he could tell, no bones had been broken. He wondered if his attacker was going to be content with having made a single devastating pass, or if this was the beginning of a duel.

"You were quick, Hasson," a voice called from the darkness. "Quicker than your wingman. But it won't do you any good."

"Who are you?" Hasson shouted as he looked for a radar bearing.

"You know who I am. I'm the Fireman."

"That's a song." Hasson kept his voice steady as he began spreading his snares and nets. "What's your real name? The one your area psychiatrist has on his books."

The darkness laughed. "Very good, Sergeant Hasson. Playing for time and trying to goad me and learn my name all at once."

"I don't need to play for time—I've already broadcast a QRF."

"By the time anybody gets here you'll be dead, Hasson."

"Why should I be? Why do you want to do this?"

"Why do you hunt my friends and ground them?"

"They're a menace to themselves and to everybody else."

"Only when you make them fly wild. You're kidding yourself, Hasson. You're a skycop, and you like hounding people to death. I'm going to ground you for good—and those nets won't help you."

Hasson stared vainly in the direction of the voice. "Nets?"

There was another laugh, and the Fireman began to sing. *"I can see you in the dark, 'cause I'm the Fireman; I can fly with you and*

you don't even know I'm there. . . ." The familiar words were
growing louder as their source drew near, and abruptly Hasson
made out the shape of a big man illuminated by the traffic streams
below and by starlight from above. He looked fearsome and inhuman in his flying gear.

Hasson yearned for the firearm that was denied to him by Brit-
ish police tradition, and then he noticed something. "Where's the
lance?"

"Who needs it? I let it go." The Fireman spread his arms and—
even in the dimness, even with the lack of spatial reference points
—it became apparent that he was a giant, a man who had no need
of weapons other than those that nature had built into him.

Hasson thought of the heavy lance plummeting down into a
crowded suburb three thousand meters below, and a cryogenic
hatred stole through him, reconciling him to the forthcoming
struggle, regardless of its outcome. As the Fireman came closer,
Hasson whirled a net in slow circles, tilting his harness to counter-
act the spin the net tried to impart to him. He raised his legs in
readiness to kick, and at the same time finished straightening out
the towline, which made Inglis's body a ghastly spectator to the
event. Hasson felt nervous and keyed up, but not particularly
afraid now that the Fireman had discarded his lance. Aerial com-
bat was not a matter of instinct; it was something that had to be
learned and practiced, and therefore the professional always had
the edge on the amateur, no matter how gifted or strongly moti-
vated the latter might be. For example, the Fireman had made a
serious mistake in allowing Hasson to get his legs fully drawn up
into the position from which the power of his thighs could be
released in an explosive kick.

Unaware of his blunder, the Fireman edged in slowly, vectoring
the lift of his harness with barely perceptible shoulder movements.
He's a good flier, Hasson thought, *even if he isn't so good on com-
bat theory and . . .*

The Fireman came in fast—but not nearly as fast as he should
have done. Hasson experienced something like a sense of luxury as
he found himself with time to place his kick exactly where he
wanted it. He chose the vulnerable point just below the visor, com-
pensated for the abrupt drop that occurred as both CG fields can-

celed out, and unleashed enough energy to snap a man's neck. Somehow the Fireman got his head out of the way in time and caught hold of Hasson's outstretched leg. Both men were falling now, but at an unequal rate, because Hasson was tethered to Inglis, whose CG field was too far away to have been canceled. In the second before they parted, the Fireman applied the leverage of his massive arms and broke Hasson's leg sideways at the knee.

Pain and shock obliterated Hasson's mind, gutting him of all strength and resolve. He floated in the blackness for an indeterminate period, arms moving uncertainly, face contorted in a silent scream. The great spiral nebula far below continued to spin, but a dark shape was moving steadily across it, and part of Hasson's mind informed him that there was no time for indulgence in natural reactions to injury. He was hopelessly outclassed on the physical level, and if life were to continue it would only be through the exercise of intelligence. But how was he to think when pain had invaded his body like an army and was firing mortar shells of agony straight into his brain?

For a start, Hasson told himself, *you have to get rid of Lloyd Inglis.* He began reeling in his comrade's body with the intention of unhooking it, but almost immediately the Fireman spoke from close behind him.

"How did you like it, Hasson?" The voice was triumphant. "That was to show you I can beat you at your own game. Now we're going to play my game." Hasson tried drawing the line in faster. Inglis's body bobbed closer and finally came within interference radius. Hasson and Inglis began to fall. The Fireman dived in on them instantly, hooked an arm around Hasson's body, and all three dropped together. The whirlpool of fire began to expand beneath them.

"This is *my* game," the Fireman sang through the gathering slipstream. *"I can ride you all the way to the ground, 'cause I'm the Fireman."*

Hasson, knowing the tactics of aerial chicken, shut out the pain from his trailing leg and reached for his master switch, but hesitated without throwing it. In two-man chicken the extinguishing of one CG field restored the other one to its normal efficacy, causing a fierce differential, which tended to drag one opponent vertically away from the other. The standard countermove was for the second man to kill his own field at the same time so that both bodies would continue to plunge downward together until somebody's nerve broke and forced him to reactivate his harness. In the present game of death, however, the situation was complicated by the presence of Inglis, the silent partner who had already lost. His field would continue negating those of the other two, regardless of what they did, unless . . .

Hasson freed an arm from the Fireman's mock-sexual embrace and pulled Inglis's body in close. He groped for the dead man's master switch but found only a smooth plaque of frozen blood. The jeweled horizons were rising rapidly on all sides now, and the circling traffic stream was opening like a carnivorous flower. Air rushed by at terminal velocity, deafeningly. Hasson fought to break the icy casting away from the switch on Inglis's harness, but at that moment the Fireman slid an arm around Hasson's neck and pulled his head back.

"Don't try to get away from me," he shouted into Hasson's ear. "Don't try to chicken out—I want to see how well you bounce."

They continued to fall.

Hasson, encumbered by his nets, felt for the buckle of the belt, which held, among other things, the towline dispenser. He fumbled it open with numb fingers and was about to release Inglis's body when it occurred to him that he would gain very little in doing so. An experienced chicken player always delayed breaking out of field interference until the last possible instant, leaving it so late that even with his harness set at maximum lift he hit the ground at the highest speed he could withstand. The Fireman probably intended going to the limit this time, leaving Hasson too disabled to prevent himself from being smashed on impact. Getting rid of Inglis's body would not change that.

They had dropped almost two thousand meters and in just a few seconds would be penetrating the crowded commuter levels. The Fireman began to whoop with excitement, grinding himself against Hasson like a rutting dog. Holding Inglis with his left hand, Hasson used his right to loop the plasteel towline around the Fireman's upraised thigh and to pull it into a hard knot. He was still tightening the knot as they bombed down into the traffic flow.   H

Lights flashed past nearby, and suddenly the slow-spinning galaxy was above them. Patterns of street lamps blossomed beneath, with moving ground cars clearly visible. This, Hasson knew, was close to the moment at which the Fireman had to break free if he was to shed enough downward velocity before reaching ground level.

"Thanks for the ride," the Fireman shouted, his voice ripping away in the slipstream. "Got to leave you soon."

Hasson switched on his flares and then jerked the towline violently, bringing it to the Fireman's attention. The Fireman looked at the loop around his thigh. His body convulsed with shock as he made the discovery that it was he and not Hasson who was linked to the dead and deadly skycop. He pushed Hasson away and began clawing at the line. Hasson swam free in the wind, knowing that the line would resist even the Fireman's giant strength. As Hasson felt his CG field spread its invisible wings, he turned to look back. He saw the two bodies, one of them struggling frantically, pass beyond the range of his flares on their way to a lethal impact with the ground.

Hasson had no time to waste in introspection—his own crash landing was about to occur, and it would require all his skill and experience to get him through it alive—but he was relieved to find that he could derive no satisfaction from the Fireman's death. Nunn and the others were wrong about him.

Even so, he thought, during the final hurtling seconds, *I've hunted like a hawk for far too long. This is my last flight.*

He prepared himself, unafraid, for the earth's blind embrace.